MIRACLE IN MILAN

MARYANN DIORIO

MaryAnn Diorio Books
www.maryanndiorio.com
"Heart-Mending Books for the Young
and the Young-at-Heart"

MIRACLE IN MILAN

by MaryAnn Diorio

Published by TopNotch Press

A Division of MaryAnn Diorio Books

PO Box 1185 Merchantville, NJ 08109

Scripture verses are taken from the King James Version of the Bible (KJV) in the public domain.

Softcover Edition: ISBN: 978-0-930037-76-5

Electronic Edition: ISBN: 978-0-930037-75-8

Library of Congress Control Number: 2021908968

Cover Design by Hannah Linder of Hannah Linder Designs

Editor: Dominic A. Diorio, M.D.

❀ Created with Vellum

To my awesome Champions . . .

You make this writing journey a joy with your love, encouragement, and support.

This one is for you!

"But if ye forgive not men their trespasses, neither will your Father forgive your trespasses."

— ~ MATTHEW 6: 15 KJV

Chapter One

egal pad in hand, Amy Torelli entered the plush office suite of the founder and president of Enson Pharmaceuticals, located in downtown Manhattan's imposing Enson Finance Building. The large, spacious office suite occupied the entire fourth floor of the old building situated on Wall Street and overlooking Midtown Manhattan. From the ceiling-to-floor window, the six Corinthian columns of the New York Stock Exchange building loomed massive and majestic directly across the street. This was the hub of world business. The epitome of financial success.

And she was privileged to be a part of it.

At least, until now.

As chief CPA for the New York City global headquarters, she'd worked hard to get to her current position. But a single word from the company president could send her whole career into a tailspin.

Holding her breath, Amy took a seat in the black leather wing chair in front of the president's desk, settled into it, and crossed her legs. If things went as she'd planned, one day she'd be the one sitting in that brown leather swivel chair behind that large mahogany desk, calling the shots just like the man sitting there now.

The constant thought of becoming the first woman president of Enson Pharmaceuticals consumed her. It was what had driven her these past six years since she'd landed the job with the top pharmaceutical company in the world. Taking over the presidency was the one thing that would enable her to say to her father—if she ever saw him again—that she'd made it without him.

That she'd made it in spite of him.

But until that day, she'd have to play her cards right. Not rock the boat. Play the corporate board game with deftness and discretion.

She clasped her hands in her lap and took a deep breath. When Wendell Conklin called an employee into his office, it could mean one of two things: either the employee would be fired, or she would receive a special assignment.

Amy braced herself. She stood between a rock and a hard place.

A rock, because being fired would confirm her occasional doubts about her competence as Enson's Chief Auditor. A hard place, because a special assignment, if unsuccessful, would arouse her worst fear: that others would think she was incompetent. A failure.

A hypocrite.

Oh, she was great at simulating confidence. Everyone said she had it all together. But truth be told, what looked like "all together" was really "falling apart." She'd grown pretty good at faking it. Faking happiness. Faking confidence. Faking success. But deep down inside, the truth ate at her.

She was broken. Blighted. A reject.

That's what betrayal did to a girl. It broke her. Crushed her spirit. Shamed her to the point that she'd wrapped herself in an impenetrable cocoon and conducted life from within its restrictive confines.

Mr. Conklin lifted his eyes from his papers and squared his gaze on her. His face looked strained, and his demeanor, tense. "Amy, there have been suspicions of embezzlement in our Italian branch office. I want you to go to Italy to find out what's going on."

Should she breathe a sigh of relief at not being fired, or should she hold her breath as she waited for the details? She opted for the middle ground.

"Enson Italia has been losing money. So much money that I'm concerned about the viability of our office there and its remaining open."

Amy raised an eyebrow. "It's that serious?"

"Yes. That serious. Something has to be done, and done quickly."

She nodded, her muscles tensing. An assignment to the Italian branch office meant she'd have to be at the top of her game. No *faux-pas*. No missteps. Only walking the tight high wire of the corporate world with a grace and finesse she didn't think she possessed. What if the whole mission fell apart?

Just as her whole world had fallen apart that day way back, when she'd realized Daddy had left for good.

Her stomach tightened as she pushed back the awful memory and forced her thoughts back to the present. "What's the plan?"

Mr. Conklin's voice was firm. "I want you to investigate. I can think of no more competent person to do so than you. Not only are you good with numbers; you're good at pegging people."

As much as Mr. Conklin's compliment flattered her, Amy doubted she deserved it. Yes, she was good with numbers. Ever since she was a kid, she'd loved their precision, their predictability, their absoluteness. Numbers could always be trusted. They were faithful. They never changed. Numbers always said what they meant and meant what they said. Numbers always told the truth; people didn't.

"When would I leave, sir?"

"I had my secretary book you on a flight to Milan that leaves tomorrow night. You have three weeks to discover the truth. That should give you enough time."

Amy tensed. Three weeks? What was Mr. Conklin thinking? Ordinary audits took at least a couple of months. But an audit involving a possible embezzlement could take a lot longer. It could even expand into years. "I'll do my best, sir."

Mr. Conklin leaned forward on his desk, his eyes trained on her. "I expect you to do better than your best. Enson Italia is on the verge of financial collapse. Whether it survives or not depends on what you discover."

Amy's stomach churned. "As I said, Mr. Conklin, I'll do my best."

He furrowed his gray bushy eyebrows that framed piercing blue eyes. "I want you to be extremely thorough on this Italian audit."

Amy stiffened. "I'm always thorough, sir."

He waved a dismissive hand. "Yes, yes. I know you're always thorough. That's the reason you're still working here." He peered at her over his horn-rimmed glasses. "But on this trip, you'll have to do more than your best, if you know what I mean."

She nodded, fear niggling at the back of her brain. Best meant nothing better. More than best meant impossible. Could she pull it off? Or would she fail? The way she'd failed as a kid. Enough to make Daddy walk out on her and Mama.

"I want you to triple-check everything. While I don't have any proof, I've got a gut feeling that our Italian division isn't being managed properly."

Amy made a note of Mr. Conklin's comment on her legal pad. She raised her gaze toward him. "May I ask what your specific concerns are, sir?"

"You can ask me anything you want, except what I had for lunch." He grimaced. "The awful thing—whatever it was—is turning my stomach sour as I speak."

"I'm sorry."

He grimaced again. "Not sorrier than I."

Mr. Conklin leaned back in his chair. "To answer your question, my specific concerns are that the Italian division is performing under par and losing money. Lots of money. I've been watching the situation for a while now, and it's not simply a question of normal economic cycles of ups and downs. My concern is that our profit margin has been demonstrating a consistently sharp downward spiral. Enough to place the entire branch in economic danger."

"Do I have *carte blanche* to look at everyone at Enson, right up to the top?"

"Absolutely." Mr. Conklin leaned forward and placed both hands on his desk. "I want you to be a detective of sorts. Look for clues as to shabby leadership, division in the ranks, and anything else that would indicate why the ship is sailing with a precarious tilt."

"That's a pretty tall order. I was planning to spend the entire three weeks auditing the books. There won't be much time for anything else."

"You've got a good, intuitive sense about people, Amy. You'll pick up vibes in the midst of the auditing, I'm sure."

But Amy wasn't sure at all. Sleuthing was out of her comfort zone. Hiding behind numbers on a computer screen was more to her liking. "I'll do my best there, too, Mr. Conklin." She didn't dare share her discomfort with him. Wendell Conklin accepted no excuses. Only positive results.

"Is there anything else, sir?" She was itching to leave.

Mr. Conklin broke into a smile. "Yes, there is. You'll be working with Ted McMasters, our American vice-president in the Italian office. Ted was the first one to pick up discrepancies in the books and to alert headquarters. He'll be of big help to you."

"Thank you."

Mr. Conklin chuckled. "I hear Ted plays a mean game of tennis. You may wish to challenge him to a match."

Amy's face grew warm at Mr. Conklin's allusion to her poor tennis-playing skills, all the while reading between the lines of his not so subtle, matchmaking comment. She smiled in spite of herself. For all of his severe demeanor, Mr. Conklin was half-executive and half-grandfather. "I'll tell Mr. McMasters you send your regards."

Mr. Conklin grew serious again. "Amy, I'm sending you into a potential quagmire. At all times, watch where you place your feet. I don't want you sinking into a morass of ugly company politics." He sighed. "Or something worse."

"I don't want to, either, Mr. Conklin." She smiled. "But what could be worse than company politics?"

He ignored her attempt at humor. "Be gentle as a dove, but wise as a serpent."

Mr. Conklin's warning quote from the Bible set Amy on edge. What did he know that he wasn't telling her? What did he suspect?

And why was he sending her into the unknown with only a warning and nothing more tangible to go on?

Amy shifted in her chair. "Is there anything more you can tell me, sir?"

He shook his head. "I wish there were. I'm going only on a hunch. A sixth sense I've developed over nearly thirty years of running Enson." He paused, a pensive look on his face. "And I hope my hunch is wrong."

Amy nodded. "I hope so, too, sir."

He stood. "One last thing. If you run into any problems while you're over there, call me right away. You have my direct number."

"Yes, thank you. I don't expect any problems, but if I do encounter them, I'll call you."

"Good."

"Is there anything else, sir?" She had an urgent desire to leave.

"No. That will be all."

Amy rose and straightened to her full height of five feet six inches. "I'll bring back a complete report when I return."

"Very good." He steadied his eyes on her. "I'm counting on you, Amy."

"I hear you, sir." What she really heard was, "There's no room for failure, Amy."

"*Bon voyage*." True to his eccentric ways, he gave her a parting military salute that reminded her of sending a soldier off to war.

A chill ran through her. Was that how Mr. Conklin viewed her mission?

"Aye, aye, Sir!" She joked, returning the salute in a vain effort to dispel her anxiety. It was clear that her work on this trip was cut out for her.

The question was, was she cut out for it?

* * * *

Back in her office, Amy opened her purse and withdrew the string of pearls she'd kept there since her mother died five years earlier. Other than Amy's memories, the pearls were her only connection to the mother who'd nurtured her and raised her alone, while holding down a full-time job. The mother Amy loved more than any other human being in the whole world.

The mother who'd died too young.

The longer Amy lived, the more she missed Mama. The more she appreciated Mama's sacrifices for her.

And the more she hated her father.

One by one, Amy tenderly fingered each pearl, blinking back the hot tears that always stung her eyes when she remembered Mama. After Daddy's cruel and senseless abandonment, Mama had tried to create as normal a life as possible for her only daughter. Without a word of complaint, Mama had hidden her own pain and had sported a continual smile. But, young as Amy was, she'd read the truth in Mama's eyes.

A lump formed in Amy's throat. If only Mama were still alive! Somehow, every time Amy fingered the pearls, she felt her presence. Mama had given them to her on her sixteenth birthday, and Amy had treasured them ever since. They were the pearls Mama had worn on her wedding day.

"Perhaps you'll decide to wear them on your own wedding day, sweetheart." Mama was the eternal optimist, despite all she'd gone through. But why would Mama want Amy to wear a string of pearls connected to a man who'd betrayed her and her daughter? Had she still loved him? Never once had she expressed any hatred toward him. Always she had prayed for him.

Far more than Amy had done. Truth be told, she could care less for what happened to her father. As far as she was concerned, he could rot in Hell. That's what he deserved for what he'd done.

Besides, no wedding day loomed in Amy's future. Not because she hadn't met anyone, but because she didn't *want* to meet anyone. She'd go it alone rather than risk being hurt again. Betrayed again. Abandoned again.

No! No man on earth was worth that.

Just then, her co-worker and best friend Sara poked her head into Amy's office. "Need a break?"

"Yeah. I could use one." Amy placed the pearls on her desk. "I was just going to grab myself a cup of coffee. Do you want one?"

"Boy, do I. I'm falling asleep at my desk."

Amy poured two cups of coffee from the pot she kept going all day long on the little table in the corner of her office and then handed one to Sara. "Have a seat." Amy motioned to the small sofa in her office. "So, I'm going to Italy on assignment."

Sara plopped down on the sofa. "Really?"

Amy nodded and then sat down next to Sara.

"So, when did all of this happen?'

"A few minutes ago. Apparently, there's trouble in our Italian office, and Mr. Conklin wants me to check it out. I'll be there for three weeks auditing the books."

"Wow! Are you excited?"

Amy took a sip of her coffee. "I have mixed feelings. I've wanted to go to Italy for a long time, especially since my grandparents came from there. But I'm nervous about the pressure it puts me under. The stress. The fear of messing up. What if things go wrong?"

"What could possibly go wrong?"

Amy looked at Sara. "I could blow it, that's what."

"You won't blow it. How can you blow an audit anyway?'

"I could miss something big."

"I think you're making a mountain out of a molehill, Amy."

"I don't know. You know Mr. Conklin. He told me he expected better than my best."

Sara laughed. "That's crazy."

"No. That's Mr. Conklin."

"Amy, you know that underneath that gruff veneer, he's really a teddy bear at heart."

"Well, I hope you're right." She sighed. "What if I botch up the whole assignment and get fired?"

"You won't get fired. You're one of Enson's prize accountants."

"You're saying that because you're my best friend."

"It has nothing to do with friendship. It's the truth." Sara squared her gaze on Amy. "What I'm most worried about is that you'll meet an Italian guy, fall in love, and get married. And then I'll be left all alone in this place."

Amy nearly choked on her coffee. "No way that's going to happen. You know how I feel about men. Ever since my father left me high and dry at the Daddy/Daughter Kindergarten party, I want nothing to do with men."

"It's not men you want nothing to do with. It's hurt."

Sara's words struck a chord.

"Well, I'd better get back to work before I'm the one who gets fired." Sara rose. "Congratulations on the assignment, girlfriend. I just know you're going to be a big hit."

Amy rose, too. "I'm glad you think so."

"I know so." Sara gave Amy a quick hug and then left.

Amy poured herself another cup of coffee and then settled in at her desk.

A shiver coursed through her body as she replaced Mama's pearls in her purse. The only thing to do was not to fail. Not to depend on anyone but herself. Then she could still hold her head up high. Still show the world she was somebody.

Still show the world she could make it without a man.

But now, she needed to focus on preparing for her trip to Italy. To tie up loose ends in the New York office before she left. To pack for three weeks away. She took a deep breath. Mr. Conklin's assignment had taken her off guard. Surprised her big time. And she hated surprises. Sudden changes in the *status quo* unnerved her, shook her equilibrium, set her on edge. She needed stability. Security. Sameness. Rocking the boat was not her way to sail.

Mr. Conklin's words echoed in her mind. "I expect more than your best, Amy." What human being could give that? For all of his grandfatherliness, Mr. Conklin was still a no-nonsense boss.

While she couldn't control the consequences of her visit to Italy, she could control her efforts on the job. She determined to do her best, if for no other reason than that her own integrity and self-respect—traits she'd come by at a heavy price—demanded it.

She'd do the right thing in the right way for Enson Pharmaceuticals and let the chips fall where they may. She'd do her best to investigate the goings on to set Mr. Conklin's mind at ease. To maintain her self-respect.

And to keep her job.

* * * *

The morning of her departure, Amy found herself seated once again in Mr. Conklin's office for an emergency meeting. His face looked strained, and his demeanor, tense.

She waited as he gathered his thoughts. A deliberate man, Conklin chose his words slowly and carefully, as she'd learned in the six years she'd worked for him. Meanwhile, she busied herself reviewing the previous day's meeting notes on the clipboard she held on her lap.

After a few moments, Mr. Conklin cleared his throat and leaned forward, his elbows on his desk, his penetrating gaze squared on her. "I've received word from Ted McMasters. Things aren't looking good. He's been reviewing the books in preparation for your audit and doesn't like what he sees."

Amy's muscles tensed. "How so?"

Mr. Conklin lowered his voice. "Ted doesn't want to jump the gun, but he's pretty sure now that someone's been fiddling with the books. He said to come prepared."

Amy's stomach hitched. Come prepared? What could that mean but major problems. Problems for which she might *not* be prepared. "Did he give you any specifics?"

"No. He said he'd give you all the details when you got there."

Amy took in a deep breath. This trip was going to be more than she'd bargained for. "What do you think is going on?"

"I don't know for sure. But I advise you to keep your eyes wide open, both while looking at the books and looking at the staff. We could have a major battle on our hands."

An alarm went off in Amy's gut. "What do you mean?"

"I mean that Enson Italia may be implicated in a global embezzlement scheme that could have international repercussions not only in Italy, but also in all of our fourteen global offices."

Her throat tightened. And she would be at the center of it all. The star of an ugly show that could air around the world.

Mr. Conklin's voice interrupted her thoughts. "What time does your flight leave?"

"At 7:30 tonight. I arrive in Milan at 8:00 in the morning. I hope to meet with Enson Italia's staff shortly thereafter."

Mr. Conklin nodded. "I'll notify Ted to set up a meeting for you." He looked at her. "Keep your wits about you, Amy. I have a feeling there's a wolf in the pack."

She took a deep breath. "Yes, sir. I will." She managed a smile. "I've wrestled with a few wolves in my life."

"Just make sure the wolf isn't dressed up like a sheep."

Amy's blood froze. The wolves she'd faced seemed minor now compared to what Mr. Conklin was implying. "I will, sir."

A sudden urge to run overwhelmed her. "Will there be anything else, sir?"

"No. That will be all." Mr. Conklin stood. "I wish you a pleasant trip, Amy." He extended his right hand. "As pleasant as possible under the circumstances."

Amy stood, her muscles tensing, and shook his hand. "Thank you. I'll keep you posted on what I find."

"Very well." Mr. Conklin's gaze steadied upon her. "I'll be praying for you, Amy."

Praying? The situation must be pretty serious for Mr. Conklin to make such a statement. "Thank you, sir."

"Sure thing."

She turned to leave. As she opened the door and entered the hallway, the impact of it all hit her with full force. Come prepared? Embezzlement? Wolves?

What had she gotten herself into? What should she do?

Should she ask to be relieved of the assignment? Not without being relieved of her job at the same time.

Amy shuddered. The next three weeks in Italy could drastically affect her career forever. If only she could turn back the clock. If only she could change her mind about the trip. If only she were as great an auditor as everyone thought she was.

Chapter Two

Theodore Edward McMasters, American-born vice-president and most eligible bachelor at Enson Pharmaceutical's Italian office in Milan, lassoed his straying thoughts back to the issue at hand and sat down at his office computer. He needed to review the books before the auditor from the States arrived. Couldn't let her think he wasn't on top of things. Maybe when she returned to the States, she'd put in a good word for him to Wendell Conklin.

Anything to keep his name in front of the man who would eventually choose his own successor.

Although Ted had frequently wondered if the presidency of Enson Global were his will or God's. As a kid, he'd had his heart set on becoming a pastor.

As Ted's eyes strained against the tiny numbers on the spreadsheet displayed across his over-sized computer screen, something didn't look right. Normally by this time of year, profits were way up. Now, although they seemed steady, in some strategic places they were far lower than usual.

His gut tensed. There it was again. That ugly sense of foreboding that his world was about to fall apart. That same sense of foreboding he'd experienced when his father had died a week before his high school graduation, and when he'd faced the enemy eye-to-eye in a surprise bombing raid in Afghanistan.

Maybe he was just overly concerned about the steep stock market dive the day before. Maybe he was just tired and seeing double. Maybe the numbers really weren't that far off from last year.

Or perhaps it was just that innate hunch—a sense he'd perfected over the past several years—that something sinister was going on. Not only in his life, but also in his company. Something evil and ugly. Something hiding beneath the surface, like a rattlesnake slithering unseen in tall grass, looking for the perfect time to strike.

He rose and began to pace the room, unable to shake the uneasy feeling that the heretofore-happy world of Enson Italia was about to crash.

And that his world was about to crash with it.

He paced the floor of his downtown office in the center of Milan's business district. Having been named vice-president of Enson's Italian branch only a year before, he'd discovered his new position to be the perfect escape from a past that continually haunted him. But even here, the respite had been only temporary. Recent increasing conflict with his staff had only confirmed his conviction that humans were not to be trusted. Especially humans who seemed trustworthy. They were the worst kind. The kind who would turn on you when you least expected it.

The way Shawna had six years earlier. Suddenly. No warning. Only a "Dear John" letter while he was on his first tour of duty in Afghanistan.

He flinched. A bullet through his heart would have hurt less. Especially since he'd been planning to ask her to marry him upon his return to Texas. Instead, he'd signed up for a second tour of duty. Better to die fighting for freedom than fighting for love.

Over the six years since, his pain had turned to hardness toward all women. A self-imposed hardness, yes. But a hardness, nonetheless. Anything to keep his already broken heart from shattering completely.

Ever since, he'd actively avoided a romantic relationship. Instead, he'd turned to conquering the world with wit rather than heart. In Ted's world, wit always won over heart, and wit was the name of the game for him. Wit had gotten him the job at Enson's

Dallas branch five years earlier. Wit had gotten him the next-to-top position as vice-president of the Italian branch office a year ago. And wit would get him to the presidency of Enson's entire global operation.

Stuffing his hands into his pockets, he took a deep breath and walked to the large second-floor window of the historic building that housed Enson's Italian headquarters. His eyes gazed on the beautiful city of Milan stretched out before him in all of its historic splendor. The city that had been his home for the past year and, if all went according to plan, would be his home until his appointment to the president's office in New York.

The lofty goal burned inside him. Not because it was something he really wanted, but because it was something he needed to prove to himself—and to the world—that he was somebody.

Ever since his father had publicly humiliated him back in high school, when Ted missed the winning shot in the state basketball championship game, he'd hidden behind a veil of humor that kept the pain at bay.

But that veil was wearing thin.

Making it to the top position at Enson Pharmaceuticals would silence his father's nagging voice inside his brain that he didn't have what it took to win, and win big-time. It would show his ex-girlfriend Shawna what a stupid mistake she'd made in dumping him.

Ted took a deep breath. Dusk had already fallen. In the distance, the magnificent spires of the *Duomo* glistened under a purple sky and a full, rising moon. On the sidewalks below, people hurried to and fro, hustling toward destinations unknown.

A sudden yearning for home gripped his heart. Despite the lovely city before him, a cushy job, and the success he'd achieved, he longed for something more. Something that would give meaning to his life beyond schmoozing clients, placating donors, and achieving quarterly quotas. Something deep and lasting.

He quickly dismissed the thought. Something "more" usually involved a relationship. And he'd already made up his mind about that.

Something brushed against his leg. Ted looked down and smiled.

The company cat, a lovely calico stray he'd found outside the office building one morning a few months prior, slinked along the edge of the windowsill. Fortunately, Ted's boss and Enson's president, Giorgio Bassetti, had allowed the creature to remain after Ted had convinced him that cats pretty much take care of themselves. Just give them a bowl of milk and they're happy.

So, Ted had given the creature a bowl of milk and named her Callie. Since then, she'd become a permanent member of the staff. Fellow employees had even set up a schedule to take turns feeding their new office mascot.

"Hey, Callie, what are you doing up here? You're supposed to be down on the first floor."

Ted picked up the furry feline and nestled her against his chest. "I won't tell anyone if you won't." Her soft fur against his neck reminded him of summer days back in Texas when, as a kid, he'd roam through the cornfields, and the silky cornstalks would brush against his face and neck.

The cat purred, rubbed her whiskers against Ted's face, and then wiggled her way out of his arms, leaping to the floor below.

Ted chuckled. "So much for cuddle time with Callie."

At the sound of a knock on the door, he turned. "Come in."

Silvia Villano, assistant to Enson Italia's president, Giorgio Bassetti, greeted him with a loaded smile and a decidedly Italian accent. "What are you still doing here? It's after closing time."

Ted stood in place, his stomach tensing yet again. "I could ask you the same question."

"I had some work to catch up on for *il presidente*." She pronounced the title with disdain. It was no secret there was something between Giorgio and his executive assistant. They hid it well, but employees had a way of seeing through company façades.

Ted removed his hands from his pockets and returned to his computer.

Silvia moved behind him. "What are you doing?"

"Nothing of major import." Silvia was as untrustworthy as the rest of them. Maybe even more so. "Just reviewing the accounting."

"Can't you leave that to the auditor who's coming tomorrow?"

Ted nodded. "I guess so. But I'm one of those people who cleans his house before the cleaning service comes."

Silvia laughed. "I'm told the Chief Auditor is a woman."

Ted's ears perked. "So?"

Silvia settled into the chair next to his. "Women can be crafty."

He turned toward her in surprise. "I would hope an auditor wouldn't be crafty, but totally honest."

"Oh, I'm not talking about math. I'm talking about method."

Ted gave Silvia a questioning glance. "I don't know what you're talking about." He turned his attention back toward the computer screen.

"I think you do." Silva rose. "If you haven't had dinner yet, perhaps we could grab something at *Domenico's Trattoria*?" Her voice was inviting.

"Thanks, but no thanks. I'll be here for a little while. I need to make sure the books are up to date before the auditor arrives."

"Very well. But don't spend too much time on them. You need your beauty sleep." Silvia smiled teasingly and gave him a little wave. "*Ciao, ciao.*"

He grunted as she left. The woman annoyed him, with her

constant attempts to win his attention. But he had to be nice to her for the sake of his already shaky relationship with his boss. Silvia was, after all, Giorgio Bassetti's assistant—and, truth be told, the one who really ran the company—and she could make things very difficult for Ted if he didn't stay on her good side.

But staying on Silvia's good side was easier said than done.

* * * *

Amy gripped the armrests of her window seat and took a deep breath as the Boeing 747 banked sharply on its final approach to Malpensa Airport. Her stomach did a somersault, landing somewhere between her heart and her throat.

Leaning her face against the window, she scanned the stunning view beneath her. In the distance, the snow-capped Alps glowed in the morning sunlight, taking her breath away. At their feet, the sun-drenched Italian landscape stretched far and wide through lush farmlands, tiny villages, and small towns. In the near distance, the city of Milan stood resplendent, bedecked like a jeweled queen on a chessboard.

Amy drew in a deep breath.

"Please fasten your seatbelts." The captain's voice jolted her out of her reverie. "We'll be landing in about five minutes."

Amy leaned back and managed a smile. In a few moments, she'd be standing on Italian soil. A dream come true, even though she'd never expected it to come true like this.

As the plane approached the landing strip, Sara's parting warning the night before at New York's JFK Airport rang in Amy's ear: "Now don't go falling in love with an Italian guy."

"Not to worry, Sara. I'm going to be in Milan for only three weeks. What can possibly happen in three weeks? You have absolutely nothing to worry about."

Sara raised an eyebrow. "Famous last words."

Amy shrugged off Sara's comment. "Besides, you know how I feel about men. I want nothing to do with them."

"I hear you, but—"

"But nothing!" Amy snapped. "I want nothing to do with men, and that settles it." Instantly she'd regretted the harsh tone of her voice. Would she ever get control of her sharp tongue? "I'm sorry for snapping at you."

Sara sighed and put a hand on Amy's shoulder. "You just don't want to be hurt again."

Sara's words hit a nerve. "Sara, I'm a pragmatist, and pragmatists aren't controlled by their feelings, whether good or bad."

"That's the reason I'm so worried. Pragmatists are the first ones to fall in love because they're not expecting to. If you fall in love with an Italian, I'll lose you forever." Eyes glistening, Sara gave her a big farewell hug. "I'll be praying for you."

Amy smiled at Sara's concern. Loyal friend that she was, Sara had only Amy's best interests at heart. But Sara needn't be concerned. Amy was going to Italy on business—so much business, in fact, she wouldn't have time for anything else.

Especially not a relationship she didn't want in the first place.

The plane touched down with a slight jolt and then glided smoothly along the runway.

Amy released a long sigh. Flying wasn't her favorite thing to do.

The plane continued to slow down on the tarmac.

"*Benvenuti a Milano*. Welcome to Milan," a bedraggled flight attendant announced with a smile. "Enjoy your stay."

Amy glanced out the window as the plane approached the terminal. When the aircraft reached a full stop, she loosened her seatbelt and stood. Already, several passengers had gathered their belongings and were making their way down the crowded aisles.

Amy retrieved her carry-on bag from the compartment above

her, gathered her shoulder bag and iPad, and waited patiently as the passengers deplaned row by row.

Holding her carry-on bag close to her side, she exited the plane and walked down the long passenger corridor leading to the main terminal. After eight hours in the air, she was glad to be on *terra firma* once again.

A clear, bright morning greeted her as she entered the terminal. The warm Italian sun shining through the large windows caressed her face. She drew in a long, deep breath of air. What a relief from the stale airplane air she'd breathed for the past eight hours!

She found baggage claim, retrieved her luggage, and passed through customs. Her next step was to look for Marco Moretti, the Enson official who would meet her at the airport. He would be carrying a large sign with her name on it. He'd take her to her hotel where she'd get freshened up before going to Enson headquarters. Good thing she'd slept for a couple of hours on the plane. There was no telling how long it would be before she could drop into bed to sleep.

She made her way into the terminal proper. Malpensa Airport bustled with life. Voices speaking several languages floated from the crowds of people who packed the area. Frazzled mothers with toddlers in tow, retirees wearing tropical shirts and sunglasses, and exuberant teens, apparently on an exchange student trip, hustled and bustled toward their individual destinations. The aroma of brewing espresso coffee filled the air.

Amy scanned the crowds for a man carrying a sign with her name on it. Her gaze finally fell on the culprit—a tall, handsome man, towering over the crowd and holding a sign that read AMY TORELLI.

That must be Marco Moretti. Weaving her way through the crowds of people, she approached the man holding the sign. Close up, he was more handsome than she'd noticed at first.

He looked flustered, annoyed even, as he kept looking around. Perhaps he was just frustrated and concerned at not being able to find her in the crowd. Or perhaps he wasn't too pleased about having to pick her up at the airport.

Finally, she stood a few feet from him. She waved her hand high in the air. "Hi!" She pointed to the sign and then to herself. "I'm the Amy Torelli on your sign. You must be Marco Moretti." She managed a smile.

He lowered the sign, his look of frustration immediately turning into a smile. "Actually, I'm Ted McMasters, vice-president of Enson's Italian branch. I'm filling in for Marco. He offers his apologies. He was called away suddenly and asked me to pick you up at the last minute."

Ted's American southern accent caught her off guard. "Oh, I hope everything's all right."

"Everything's fine. It turned out to be a broken pipe in his house that was leaking water into the basement. But he's got everything under control now."

"Good. Glad to hear it."

Ted showed her his company ID and extended a hand. "Welcome to Italy."

Amy smiled and shook his hand. It felt warm and strong. "Thanks. Nice to meet you, Ted."

"Likewise." Ted hesitated, seemingly unsure of what to say next.

Amy sensed his discomfort. "So, you're American?"

He nodded proudly. "Yes. Born and bred in West Texas."

Amy couldn't believe it. "No way!"

"Yes way. In a little town called Odessa."

"I know Odessa."

Ted gave her a surprised look. "You do? How do you know Odessa?"

"I'm originally from West Texas, too. In fact, we're neighbors.

My family lived not far from Odessa, in Midland, until I was ten, and then, to my great dismay, we moved to Peoria, Illinois."

Ted shook his head and laughed. "That doesn't count. Once a Texan, always a Texan."

"I agree."

Ted looked up at the sign he'd been carrying. "Well, I guess I won't need this anymore. He tossed it into the nearest trashcan.

As they walked in the direction of the parking lot, he turned toward her. "I can't believe that not only are you from Texas, but you're also from a small town near mine. What are the odds of that?"

"I'll have to get out my calculator to figure that one out."

Ted chuckled. "But you're a CPA, aren't you? You should be able to figure that one out without a calculator."

Amy flinched. Was he joking with her or challenging her expertise?

Ted didn't give her a chance to reply. "Well, whatever the odds, this feels more like a family reunion to me than a visit from an auditor."

And, as much as Amy hated to admit it, it felt more like a family reunion to her as well. Meeting a fellow Texan—and a handsome, witty one, at that—had caught her off guard. And being caught off guard made her feel uncomfortable. Out of control.

Vulnerable.

And vulnerable was one thing she could not afford to be. Especially when it came to men.

* * * *

Maybe it was homesickness, or maybe it was the unexpected, pleasant effect Amy Torelli had had on him upon meeting her, but Ted McMasters' heart felt a bit unsettled.

No. A *lot* unsettled.

He'd brought her to her hotel and waited in the lobby while she freshened up for the meeting. The female New York CPA now sitting to his right in the passenger seat of his Fiat 500 was a far cry from the woman he'd imagined as Enson's auditor. He'd pictured a stocky, gray-haired, middle-aged woman in sturdy black pumps, wearing a formless business suit and thick bifocals. A woman who'd think like a man, work like a man, and not pose any emotional threat to him.

Instead, Enson's stunning and captivating auditor had set his heart reeling the instant he saw her and threatened to topple it off its seemingly secure perch.

But he'd caught it just in time.

No woman would ever derail him again, no matter how beautiful or captivating she was. His mind was made up. He'd spent the last six years since Shawna's rejection avoiding all emotional ties with women. The potential pain of love wasn't worth the risk. Now or ever. He'd steel himself against Amy Torelli with every fiber of his being.

And then some.

But it might turn out to be the most difficult challenge of his life. After all, having to work with her every day for the next three weeks could do him in, if he let it. He'd have to be continually on his guard. Continually keeping his heart shut to her beauty, her charm, and her engaging personality. Continually saying no to the temptation to open his heart to love again.

No. Love was absolutely out of the question for Ted McMasters. A person could take only so much rejection before it became outright stupid to risk rejection again.

And if nothing else, Ted McMasters was not stupid.

Amy's voice interrupted his internal monologue. "Thanks for waiting while I checked in at the hotel."

"Sure thing."

"So, fill me in on what's happening with the books?"

"Oh, yeah. I guess Mr. Conklin told you we're losing income big-time here in the Italian branch. I haven't been able to figure it out. Our sales are higher than they've ever been, but our profit margins have dropped drastically. There's got to be a leak somewhere."

"How long has this been going on?"

"My guess is quite a while, although I just discovered the discrepancies recently."

"Hmm. Who takes care of your books?"

"Giorgio Bassetti, our president, is in charge of finances and supervises, but his personal assistant, Silvia Villano, actually keeps the books."

"And you? What's your role with the books?"

"I make entries whenever different departments give me their receipts."

"Don't all receipts go to one person?"

"No. Some receipts come to me, others go to Silvia, and others to Giorgio."

"I see."

At the serious tone of her voice, Ted glanced at Amy. The look on her face told him she wasn't pleased with the bookkeeping setup. "I take it you don't like the way we're handling the receipts, do you?"

"Well, at first glance, it looks as though your system could stand a makeover. But first, I want to take a close look at the company ledgers before I make any judgments."

Ted liked her deliberative approach. Amy didn't jump to conclusions. She wanted to get all the facts first.

She changed the subject. "So, tell me about this meeting we're going to."

He was grateful to get off the topic of the ledgers. "It's a way to welcome you formally to the Italian branch. Mr. Conklin thought it would be a good idea for the entire staff to meet you upfront and for you to meet them."

Amy yawned. "Well, I hope I can stay awake through the meeting. My internal clock is still on New York time."

"Hey, I hear you. Having made that transatlantic flight a few times myself, all I ever wanted upon arrival was to get some sleep."

Amy yawned again. "You got that right."

"I'll tell you what. As soon as the meeting is over, I'll whisk you away to your hotel so you can take a long afternoon nap."

"That sounds great, but I'd hoped to get started on the audit today. I have only three weeks to complete it. I want to allow myself enough time in case I hit any snags."

"But if you catch up on your sleep today, you'll be wide awake and ready to go tomorrow." He glanced at her and smiled.

"Your advice sounds tempting. I just might take it."

Ted turned onto the street where Enson Italia headquarters were located. "We're not far from the office. Are you nervous?"

"Just a little."

"Don't worry, you'll be a hit for sure."

She gave him a sidelong glance. "What makes you say that?"

Heat rose to Ted's face. "I just have this gut feeling you will." He dared not tell her she'd already made a huge hit with him.

"I wish I had the same gut feeling."

"Just give 'em the old Texas smile and handshake. That'll do it every time."

Amy laughed, and the sound of her laughter rang like music in his ears.

He pulled into the employee parking lot behind the Enson building. "Here we are! Welcome to Enson Italia! It's not as imposing as the New York office, but it's a nice place, nonetheless."

Ted opened the passenger door for Amy and then led her to

the back entrance of the building. As he opened the door of the historic building to allow Amy to enter before him, the waft of her perfume floated across his nostrils.

He swallowed hard. The next three weeks were going to be the most difficult three weeks of his entire life.

Chapter Three

S ilvia Villano was no fool. But she'd played Giorgio Bassetti for one for far too long. Feigning love for him, she'd extracted a nice lifestyle from the company's pecuniary pockets— with Giorgio's tacit approval—stashing away a substantial fortune for herself over the ten years she'd worked for him.

But now that she was approaching her thirtieth birthday—and now that Ted McMasters had joined the Italian team—it was time for a change.

She stood in front of the mirror in her lavish, two-thousand-square-foot apartment in the wealthy community of Basiglio, just outside the city. She'd moved in, compliments of Bassetti. In fact, mostly everything she owned was compliments of Giorgio Bassetti. Her Lamborghini. Her two mink coats. Her diamond and emerald rings. Giorgio had given her the good life. And she'd paid an exorbitant price for it in terms of personal freedom, peace, and morality.

But now it was time for a change.

It was time to think about the rest of her life. Did she want to reach old age without a husband and children? Without the joys of family life? Without the lively chatter and laughter of grandchildren? Did she want to miss out on the blessings of growing old with someone who loved her for who she was, not for what she could give him?

A lump caught in her throat.

With the arrival of Ted McMasters at Enson Italia the year before, Silvia's interests had shifted from her boss to his new vice-president. Yet, all of her efforts thus far to attract the handsome young American had failed miserably. He wasn't like most men she'd known. Flirtatious. Fun-loving.

And fleeting.

No. He was solid, stable, and secure. And at her age, she wanted solid, stable, and secure. She was tired of living on the prowl. Tired of playing the cat-and-mouse game. Tired of yielding to the demands of a man thirty years her senior.

Blinking back uncommon tears, she removed a stray piece of lint from her red cashmere sweater and brushed aside a rebellious red curl from her forehead. The slight crows' feet around her chocolate brown eyes made her muscles tense. She wasn't getting any younger. She'd need to make a move soon if she didn't want to live the rest of her life alone.

And what better place to make a move than with Ted McMasters.

Especially now that the Italian office was being shaken up. As Bassetti's personal assistant, Silvia knew exactly what was going on at Enson Italia. For a nice price, she'd convinced Giorgio to let her in on the rumblings.

And, as usual, he'd acquiesced to her charms. Quite easily, in fact.

He'd told her that the upcoming visit by the chief auditor of the New York office was no routine visit. The head honchos back in the States had gotten wind of something, and they planned to check it out.

A shudder went through her. If the auditor discovered the truth, Giorgio Bassetti would be dead meat.

And she?

She didn't want to think about that. She'd get out of the game before it was too late. In fact, she'd even planned for that eventuality. But she'd never thought she'd see the day when she might have to implement her plan.

Silvia gave one last look at her flashy red hair, darkly lined eyes, and well-endowed body. She then turned from the mirror and grabbed her white leather jacket. She had only fifteen minutes to get to the meeting where Ted would introduce the visiting auditor from the New York office.

A twinge of jealousy pricked her at the thought that Ted had been summarily dispatched to the airport to pick up the young woman. Silvia had seen her picture on the headquarters' website and couldn't deny she was a beauty.

Would Ted think so, too?

Silvia swallowed hard. Not if she had anything to do with it.

Perhaps she needed to make that move sooner rather than later.

Before Amy Torelli stole Ted McMasters from Silvia's shaky grip.

* * * *

Amy scanned the large, well-lit conference room situated on the spacious first floor of the Enson Italia Building. Thick Ionic columns stood at each of the four corners of the room, framing it with classic style and a bit of pomposity. On one side, a series of arched, Romanesque-style windows covered almost the entire wall. Above the windows, an arched ceiling with a skylight in the center of it cast a soft glow upon the people in the room. On the opposite wall, a huge Renaissance painting by some nondescript artist graced the area, accentuated by a large, ornate wall sconce on either side of it.

Seven men and five women sat around the long, rectangular conference table. At the head sat a broad-shouldered man who most likely was Giorgio Bassetti, his lips a straight line, his eyes narrow. To his right sat one of the women—a shapely redhead with eyes glued to Amy. She held a pad of paper and a pen in her hand, as though ready to take notes. From Ted's earlier description, the woman must be Silvia Villano, Bassetti's personal assistant. Hers and Bassetti's were the only faces without a smile. The others in the room sported broad, welcoming smiles.

Amy made a mental note of their reactions, remembering Mr. Conklin's compliment about her discerning powers of observation and his admonition to use them. She placed these two—Bassetti and Silvia—on her watch-closely list. Clearly, they were on a different team. The opposing team. And it was obvious they frowned upon her visit. She'd make it her goal to discover why.

The men stood as Amy entered the room, while the women remained seated.

Taking her elbow, Ted looked toward Amy and smiled. "Ladies and gentlemen, I would like to introduce to you Miss Amy Torelli, Chief Auditor from our New York office. Let's give her a warm Italian welcome."

The roomful of people burst into applause. Except for Giorgio and Silvia. They made only a show of applause, their hands barely touching each other amid the loud clapping of the others, their faces remaining blank.

Another mental note.

Tension pulled at Amy's throat as she stood in front of the room, wishing Ted's introduction would be over quickly so she could hide from the accolades, and especially from Silvia's hot stares. Amy hated being in the limelight. Hated being the center of attention, with all eyes focused on her. It was the same awful feeling she'd experienced when her Kindergarten classmates had gathered around her to ask her why her Daddy had not shown up for the Daddy-Daughter Day. She'd wanted to run and hide.

She pushed aside the searing memory.

Chatter filled the room as the staff made their way toward her to shake her hand. "*Benvenuta in Italia!* Welcome to Italy!" One after another, they greeted her warmly, speaking in stilted English, with heavy Italian accents.

Amy greeted them politely, thanking each one for

welcoming her in such a kind and special way. Perhaps she imagined it, but one gentleman looked at her and then gave Ted a sly wink. Remembering her Nonna, Amy smiled. Nonna used to say Italians were matchmakers at heart. And, as Nonna would often remind her, they were usually right in their matchmaking.

After the greetings, Giorgio Bassetti brought the meeting to order. Amy listened intently, absorbing as much as she could of Enson Italia's proceedings, while seeking to understand its culture at the same time. She took extensive notes, which she'd refer to later in the quiet of her hotel room.

The meeting finally ended and, as meetings go, was quite productive. But by one o'clock p.m., jet lag had finally caught up with her. When invited to participate in an afternoon tour of Milan, Amy politely declined, kindly requesting a raincheck.

Ted approached her. "I'll take you back to your hotel. You must be exhausted." He smiled. "In case you haven't figured it out yet, I've been assigned to be your personal escort during your stay here."

A thrill shot through Amy's soul, but she forced herself to suppress it.

Before she could reply, the attractive redhead sidled up to Ted and took him by the arm.

Jealousy coursed through Amy's veins, surprising her. She had no claims to Ted McMasters. What right did she have to feel jealous?

Silvia brushed closely against Ted, but he pulled away. "Ted, my friend," Silvia cooed. "Have you forgotten about our lunch date?"

Ted's jaw squared. "Excuse me, Silvia." He looked sheepishly at Amy. "Amy, this is Silvia Villano, Giorgio Bassetti's personal assistant. Silvia, this is Amy Torelli, a fellow Texan."

Amy recognized her as the woman who'd had the wooden

look on her face during the whole meeting, the one who'd remained in her seat when the others came up to greet her.

Like a scanner scanning the details of a document, Silvia eyed Amy up and down, all the while clinging to Ted's arm.

Amy read the discomfort in Ted's eyes. To her great surprise, she felt an overpowering urge to tear the woman away from him. How dare she take such liberties!

"So, you are from Texas?" Silvia's lips coiled into a judgmental smile. "The land of the cowboys?" Her Italian accent rolled over the words with mocking contempt.

The hair at the nape of Amy's neck stood on edge. "Yes, I'm from Texas, but I now live in New York City."

"But you don't look like a city girl." Silvia emphasized the word *city*, as though anything not related to city life were beneath one's dignity.

Loosing his arm from Silvia's grip, Ted broke in. "Amy, I think I'd better take you back to your hotel. You're going to need all the rest you can get to handle the full schedule ahead of you these next three weeks."

"I'll come with you." Silvia tugged on Ted's arm. "I don't want you to be lonely on the trip back." She smiled a seductive smile.

Ted shot a troubled glance at Amy, and then back at Silvia. "It's not necessary, Silvia. I won't be long."

Silvia curled her lower lip into a pout. "Very well, Ted. Whatever you say."

Ted motioned Amy toward the door. "Let's go."

As Amy left, she glanced backward just in time to see the fire raging in Silvia's jealous brown eyes.

* * * *

The next morning, Enson Italia had a rental car for Amy's use at the entrance to her hotel. The day was clear and the sun bright. Despite a restless night of sleep, followed by a quick breakfast of black espresso and a *brioche*, Amy was ready to start her new assignment.

Using her cell phone GPS, she drove the few blocks to the Enson office amid the sounds of honking horns and shouting food peddlers. Milan traffic made New York City traffic feel like Kindergarten. All along the way, people crossed the street without looking for approaching cars. At one point, she almost struck an elderly man who suddenly stepped down from the curb right in front of her, oblivious to his surroundings. At another point, a triple-decker bus pulled up too close beside her, nearly scraping the driver's side of the tiny rental car. By the time she arrived at Enson headquarters, her nerves were shot and her emotional equilibrium off kilter. Not a good way to begin her first day on the job.

She parked in the parking lot assigned to employees and made her way to the building. She braced herself. Despite Mr. Conklin's warning, Amy had already gotten embroiled in company politics against her wishes, and she hadn't even started her auditing assignment yet. At times like these, she wished she lived a simple life in a quiet, out-of-the-way town in Texas.

She sighed. Maybe someday.

But real life now stared her in the face. And she had no choice but to deal with it.

First on her agenda was to report to Giorgio Bassetti's office. He had expressed his desire the previous day that she meet with him before beginning her audit.

His request had made her uncomfortable. She'd sensed something evil about the man. Something false. Fake. Hypocritical. As though he lived two separate lives.

Giorgio personally welcomed her into his office suite where

two secretaries sat typing away at their computers. They greeted her cordially and then resumed their typing.

"This way, Ms. Torelli." Giorgio led her into his private office and shut the door. It was a modest office, as far as offices go. Nothing like Mr. Conklin's plush space in the downtown Manhattan headquarters. A medium-sized window overlooked a narrow street with another office building on the opposite side. In one corner of the office space stood a large plant about the size of a small fig tree. On a credenza behind the desk was a picture of two small children sitting on either side of a lovely woman who looked to be in her late thirties. Very likely Giorgio's wife and children.

"Please, sit down." Giorgio pointed to a small sitting area in the opposite corner furnished with two barrel chairs and a small coffee table.

Amy took the chair to the right and sat down. Her muscles tensed.

Bassetti sat down in the chair across from her, crossed his legs, and folded his hands in his lap. "First of all, I want to thank you for making the long trip to Italy to help us."

Dare she say she'd had no choice but to lose her job if she'd refused? "I'm glad to do what I can."

Bassetti cleared his throat. "I don't know how much you know, but Enson Italia is on the verge of bankruptcy."

Amy nodded. "Yes, Mr. Conklin explained as much to me."

"Then you know that we are in a precarious situation. The future of our Italian operation depends on your discovering what is going on."

Amy stiffened. There it was again. The burden of responsibility resting squarely on her shoulders. A burden she didn't like at all. She hated having the ball in her court. "Yes, I understand." She squared her gaze on him. "So, what are your thoughts on the problem?" She loved to toss the ball back to where it belonged.

Bassetti shifted in his chair. "Frankly, I don't know."

Amy sensed he was lying. "But surely, from your perspective as president, you have some idea, do you not?" His dodging annoyed her.

Bassetti squirmed. "All I can say is that we have discovered some expenses that do not align with our expenditure categories and that seem to have no correlation with our normal business expenses."

"Has any one investigated those unusual expenses?"

Bassetti's eyes narrowed. "That is what you are here to do." His voice was curt.

Amy took in a deep breath. She didn't like being brought up short. It was a common male tactic to shift blame and the burden of proof. Especially on to women. And she would not stand for it. "Very well. Then may I assume I have free reign to conduct any investigation I deem necessary to get to the bottom of this?"

He hesitated, but only briefly. "You do."

Amy made a mental note of his brief hesitation. "Thank you very much, Mr. Bassetti. I'll get to work right away. This is a big job to complete in only three weeks."

"I understand."

Amy raised her chin. "One last thing."

"Yes?"

"I need a list of everyone who has access to the books."

"Only three of us: I myself, Ted, our vice-president, and Silvia, my personal assistant."

Just as Ted had told her. "Do your by-laws permit personal assistants to have access to the company's books?"

Giorgio shifted in his chair. "Such permission is not explicitly stated in our by-laws."

"Then I suggest that you immediately add a clause to that

effect to prevent future problems. The fewer people who have access to the books, the better."

"Silvia is quite trustworthy."

Amy's hair went up on the nape of her neck. "It is not a person's trustworthiness that is the issue, Mr. Bassetti. It is proper and legal company protocol. For instance, would you give your trustworthy custodian access to your books?"

Giorgio's eyes became slits. "I get your point, Ms. Torelli."

Amy hadn't intended to be sarcastic. "I'm simply trying to help. I've seen too many companies taken down because they did not have specific instructions as to who had access to the books. And the wrong people were given access."

Giorgio nodded. "I can assure you that Silvia is a woman of great integrity. I believe that your investigation will bear out that fact."

Amy rose. "I hope so, sir. But realize that I must begin with the assumption that anyone could be guilty of indiscretion in an auditing case, be that indiscretion intentional or not."

Giorgio stood to his feet as well. "Please let me know as soon as you have any leads."

"I will, sir."

But first Amy would report any suspicious findings to Vice-President Ted McMasters. So far, maybe because he was an American and a fellow Texan, he was the only person she felt she could trust to tell her the truth.

But even so, she determined to be careful.

Very careful.

Chapter Four

Ted eagerly glanced at the clock. Amy would be arriving in ten minutes for their first official meeting regarding the audit. He ran his fingers through his hair, trying to keep his pulse from racing. The young auditor from New York was fast taking hold of his heart.

He glanced at the wall clock and then turned toward the mirror behind his desk. He smoothed back his hair and wiped a speck of dust off his navy blue, pinstriped suit jacket. To his dismay, he found himself wanting to look extra good for his special guest from New York.

A notepad on his desk listed the items he needed to review with Amy. First on the list involved Silvia and Giorgio. Both of them had expressed displeasure with the New York office's insistence on the audit, but they were over-ruled by Mr. Conklin after Ted reported his concerns to him.

Second on the list was a question about how he could best help Amy while she was here. Never having participated in an audit, he didn't quite know what to expect. So, he would let her lead as to what she needed from him and when.

Third on the list was to remind Amy that he would be her official tour guide during her stay. If, that is, she wanted a tour guide. Three weeks would fly by, and he wanted to make sure that her stay in Milan was not only productive but also pleasurable.

Of course, his motives were not purely selfless. On the contrary, there was a lot of selfishness in them. He wanted to get to know her better before she returned to New York. Something inside him—maybe it was God—compelled him not to let Amy get away without any attempt on his part to establish a simple friendship with her. But not more than that. Even that level made him nervous. After all, it was a small step from friendship to love.

He tore the list from the notepad, folded it, and placed it in his shirt pocket. Then he turned to his computer to check yesterday's sales quotas. Amy might want a report on them. As usual, sales were good. Nothing much had changed in that department, except that sales seemed higher than usual. Yet, the Italian branch was losing money. It didn't make sense.

As he scanned through the sales quotas, his mind kept drifting to Amy. Despite her very professional demeanor, there was something sweet and innocent about her that reminded him of a happier, carefree time. A time when life was simple and clean and pure. For the last few months, he'd had an increasing desire to recapture that simple time. Ever since Amy's arrival, that desire had increased exponentially. She'd stirred something in him that made his present life seem empty and pointless.

But what would a beautiful, intelligent woman like Amy want with a guy like him anyway? She probably had the brightest and the best falling at her feet, and she could take her pick of any one of them.

No. Amy Torelli deserved much better than he could offer her. She deserved a guy who was her equal in confidence, accomplishment, and charm.

A guy who commanded respect and admiration.

Not the guy who was responsible for his basketball team's loss of the state championship. Not the guy whose dad had called him a loser. Not the guy whose girlfriend had dumped him while he was in Afghanistan.

Ted shook his head. He might not be the sharpest knife in the drawer, but of one thing he was certain: he had to know more about Amy Torelli.

* * * *

Amy left Giorgio Bassetti's office a bit wiser about what she was up against. Giorgio seemed to be hiding something behind his sophisticated façade. Although she couldn't quite put her finger on it yet, she knew it was there. Mr. Conklin was right. She had a sixth sense for discerning things beneath the surface. And there was definitely something beneath the surface of Giorgio Bassetti. She made a mental note to keep a vigilant eye on him.

Her next appointment was with Ted. A quick stop at the restroom before reporting to his office gave Amy an opportunity to collect herself and to apply an extra touch of lipstick. She pressed her lips together in a vain attempt to quiet the anticipation in her heart.

Truth be told, her nerves were a bit on edge at having to work with Ted McMasters. He wasn't what she'd expected. He was far more. He was young, single, and handsome. And from her home state of Texas, to boot. He possessed a confidence about himself that she lacked, and he also had a sense of humor, something she'd never been able to cultivate after her father's abandonment.

Amy sighed. What if Ted discovered she wasn't all Enson made her out to be?

She caught herself. What difference did it make what Ted McMasters thought about her? She wasn't here to please him. She was here to audit the books.

Taking a deep breath, she grabbed her purse, left the restroom, and headed toward Ted's office. It was located on the second floor, at the far end of the hall.

She walked briskly, her spiked heels clicking loudly against the white marble floor. A ray of sunshine from the large Romanesque window at the end of the hall flooded the hallway.

Just before she reached Ted's office, Silvia exited one of the side offices and intercepted Amy's path. "Well, if it isn't the famous Amy Torelli from the New York office?" A fake smile plastered Silvia's face.

Amy drew in a deep breath. Silvia was going to be the thorn

in her flesh on this assignment. Amy mustered her most cheerful voice. "Good morning, Silvia!"

Silvia lifted her chin. "*Buon giorno*." She gave Amy the once-over. "So, I see you are headed to Mr. McMasters' office."

"Yes." Amy almost gave Silvia the reason but then stopped herself. The woman was not to be trusted. The less Amy said to her, the better.

"I must warn you about Mr. McMasters."

Silvia's comment rubbed Amy the wrong way. It indicated disloyalty on Silvia's part toward Ted. Or, perhaps, an attempt to discredit him in Amy's eyes for Silvia's benefit. Amy waited politely.

"He is a man who does not understand our Italian ways."

"Oh? And what are your 'Italian' ways, if I may be so bold as to ask?" Amy one-upped her. "I certainly would like to understand them while I am here so that I may better do my job and promote good intercultural relationships at the same time." Amy drove the verbal spike into Silvia with relish and offered her a genuine smile.

Silvia gave her a haughty look. "The best way to explain them is to say they are 'caught' rather than 'taught'."

"I see." Amy pursed her lips. "Then I will simply have to practice my catching." She gave Silvia her best smile. "And now, if you will excuse me, Miss Villano, I have an appointment with Mr. McMasters." With that, Amy left Silvia to her angry self, turned on her heels, and continued down the hall, her insides seething.

This Silvia woman was one of the wolves in sheep's clothing Mr. Conklin had warned her about. Amy could sense it in her bones. Only, Silvia's clothing was anything but sheep-like. The woman was up to no good. Silvia's contempt toward Amy was palpable. So palpable Amy could cut it with a knife.

But why the contempt? Amy had a pretty good hunch, but

she'd have to confirm it. Her hunch was that Silvia had her eye on Ted and that Amy was a threat to her. If only Silvia knew she had nothing to worry about. Amy did not have her eye on Ted. But one thing Amy did have was her protective instinct to watch the back of a fellow Texan. She would never relinquish that.

* * * *

Silvia Villano's stomach churned as she sat at her computer in her office adjacent to Giorgio's. She was shaking too much to concentrate on her work. The green-eyed monster was ripping her insides apart, and all she could do was succumb to its vicious attack.

Her recent encounter with Amy in the hallway had left her with a feeling of vulnerability she'd never experienced before. All of her life, she'd out-shown every other woman in her path when it came to beauty and allure. She'd flattened the best female competition Italy could offer. She'd captured the heart of every man she'd set her eyes on.

Except for Ted McMasters.

He was like a slippery eel. Whenever she thought she'd had him securely in her grasp, he'd escaped her tenacious grip. Nothing seemed to work with him. Had she already lost her touch? And only at age thirty?

To make matters worse, now that Amy Torelli had arrived, Silvia's chances of catching Ted were slim. Very slim. She'd noticed the way Ted looked at Amy, and the way Amy looked at him. They were looks of budding love. Real love. And Silvia hated that.

Hot tears stung her eyes. Yes, they were tears of jealousy, but mixed in with them were tears of sorrow. Sorrow at having been born out of wedlock to a drug-addicted mother and without a father to raise her. Sorrow at having been left alone to fend for herself as a young child while her mother worked the streets. Sorrow at having had to make it all alone in the world.

And so it was that she'd latched on to Giorgio Bassetti when he'd offered her the job at Enson. It was far better than working as a cleaning woman for the rich. A job she'd done for several years before meeting Giorgio at a local bar.

He'd taken her under his wing. Trained her.

And made her his mistress.

Her tears were also tears of self-loathing. Truth was that Silvia Villano hated herself. Hated the woman she'd become. Sure, she had all the creature comforts she could ever want. But she didn't have what she wanted most: a family.

When things between her and Giorgio started to grow stale, she'd turned to Ted McMasters. She'd had her eye on him ever since his arrival from the States. He'd seemed an easy target. In Italy, American men were known for their naïveté. Silvia had thought Ted would be a pushover. But he'd surprised her with his solid character and resistance to her wiles. He'd seen through her, and he'd wanted nothing of her.

Yet, she'd persisted, trying new tactics, new wiles. For a short while, he seemed to be coming around. Or at least she hoped so.

But Amy Torelli's arrival had messed up all of her plans.

Silvia wiped away her tears with her fingertips. She would not allow Amy Torelli to steal her future from her. There had to be a way to keep Amy and Ted from getting together. And Silvia would find it, no matter what the cost.

Chapter Five

When Amy reached Ted's office, she took hold of the doorknob and, bracing herself, opened the door and entered.

The receptionist area was small in comparison to Giorgio's office, but it was tastefully decorated. A young woman sat facing the front door, her eyes fixed on her computer.

When Amy entered, she looked up. "*Buon giorno*. How may I help you?"

Amy smiled. "*Buon giorno*. My name is Amy Torelli. I'm here to meet with Mr. McMasters."

The woman rose. "Ah, yes, Miss Torelli. Mr. McMasters is expecting you." She ushered Amy down a short hallway to Ted's office and stood at the open doorway. "Mr. McMasters, Miss Amy Torelli is here to meet with you."

"Yes. Please tell her to come in."

The woman motioned for Amy to enter and then left.

"Hey, Amy!" Ted stood and gave her a proper Texas welcome to his office: a big smile and a strong handshake. His look was approving. Although he didn't say it, he seemed to like the sapphire blue dress she'd chosen to wear today since he scanned her from head to toe in a quick instant. "I've been looking forward to meeting with you."

She wouldn't dare say she had, too. Very much so. "It's good to see you again." After her strained encounter with Silvia, Ted was a balm to her spirit.

"Likewise." He smiled. "So how are you doing on your first day on the job?"

Not wishing to come across as a complainer, she hesitated to tell him about her recent encounter with Silvia in the hallway, "Rip rarin' to go."

Ted laughed. "Well, wahoo! Ride 'em, bronco! You make it feel like downhome Texas!"

The sound of his laugh went right to her heart. Ted McMasters was one guy who could put a crack in her emotional wall if she'd let him.

But she wouldn't let him. Ever!

"Would you like a cup of coffee? I just made a fresh pot."

"Espresso?"

"No, I make my good, old Texas brew. My mom has it shipped to me every couple of months."

Amy laughed. "Well, aren't you the spoiled son!"

"I'd say so." His smile flashed brilliant and warmed her heart.

She sat down in the nearest chair. Ted's office was furnished in a simple, contemporary style. Sleek lines. Minimal *accoutrements*. A large map of their home state hung on one wall.

"Nice office. Especially the map." She hesitated. "Do you miss Texas?"

He poured two cups of coffee. "I do. Most of all, I miss my mom and my younger brother."

Dare she ask about his father?

"My dad died when I was in high school."

It seemed as though Ted had read her thoughts.

"Oh, I'm so sorry." Amy didn't know which was worse. Losing a father to death or losing a father to abandonment.

Ted brushed off her compassion. "No sweat. I got over it."

She stopped short. His feeble attempt at bravado did not escape her. Something painful lurked under Ted's seemingly flippant words, and she'd make it her goal to find out what.

He handed her a cup of coffee and sat down across from her. "Cream and sugar are on the coffee table."

"Thanks." Amy stirred two teaspoons of sugar into her coffee and then added some cream.

Ted's gaze trained on her. "Why do I get homesick every time I talk with you?"

She smiled. "Must be my Texas blood."

His gaze lingered on her for a brief moment.

Heat rose to Amy's face. She took a sip of her coffee to hide her emotion and then changed the subject. "So, I'm all ears to hear what's going on here in the Italian branch. From your point of view, that is. Mr. Conklin and Mr. Bassetti already gave me theirs."

Ted retrieved the list of discussion topics from his shirt pocket. "I've written down three things I need to discuss with you upfront. But first, tell me how your meeting with Giorgio went."

"Well, I would describe it as strained." She took another sip of her coffee. "It was obvious we didn't hit if off very well. Actually, we didn't hit it off at all."

"I can't say I'm surprised. Giorgio is a tough cookie to read. He keeps his cards close to his chest."

"I figured as much. He confirmed what you said, that Silvia has access to the books."

"Yes. It's something I don't agree with, but I can't do much about it."

"Why not?"

"Because I'm not the head honcho around here." He laughed. "Although one day I'm going to be president of the entire Enson Operation."

Amy widened her eyes. "Oh, really? Well, you'll have to wait until I step down from that position."

Now it was Ted's turn to widen his eyes. "So, you want to be president, too?"

She nodded. "It's been my burning desire for quite a while now."

"Well, I must say I have some heavy competition then."

Amy smiled at the compliment. "We'll have a run-off. Winner treats loser to dinner."

"Great! What's your favorite restaurant?"

Ah! So, Ted liked to tease, did he? She'd show him he'd met his match in her. "I think you'd better reserve that question for the day I'm hired over you. Then you can tell *me* what *your* favorite restaurant is."

The verbal repartee sent sparks flying between them.

Ted jumped right in. "No way! You're looking at the future president of Enson International. Take a long, hard look, Amy Torelli, and don't forget this face." Ted gave three thrusts of his right index finger toward his face. "One day you will be looking at it from the other side of the mahogany desk in the president's office in Manhattan."

Amy gave him a mischievous smile. "We'll see about that, Mr. McMasters."

The atmosphere in the air had changed. Amy sensed it. Something had happened during their playful exchange, something that had shifted their relationship in a new direction. A direction she feared and had to avoid.

She swallowed hard and sipped her coffee again. The warm brew felt good going down her throat. Unnerved by what had just happened between her and Ted, she brought the conversation back to more serious matters. "I asked Giorgio if your by-laws allow personal assistants access to the books, and he said that the by-laws aren't clear about the matter."

"He's right. They aren't. And that's a huge problem."

"I agree." Amy sighed. "But we can't do anything about that now. The fact is that Silvia has already had access to the books. So, we need to look for evidence of fraud, wherever that may lead."

"Where do we start?"

"Let's start with the three things you want to discuss with me."

"Okay, first off. I think you should know that Giorgio and Silvia were none too happy about your visit."

Amy raised an eyebrow. "Really? I was under the impression that Giorgio had requested the audit."

"No. Actually, I was the one who contacted Mr. Conklin. Before that, I had expressed my concerns to Giorgio, but he assured me that he had everything under control. Nevertheless, my gut told me I should contact New York. I was concerned about some unusual entries I'd discovered, and I thought we needed an outside, objective evaluation of the books."

"Hmm. I see." Amy wrapped both hands around her coffee mug to warm them. "That sheds a whole new light on things." She pondered the situation a moment. "What's your next point?"

"Point number two is how can I best help you while you're here?"

If only she could confess to him her concern about messing up. About failing Mr. Conklin. Enson. And, most of all, herself. "You can best help me by providing whatever information I need to get the job done. For example, I'll need copies of purchase orders, receipts. That kind of stuff."

Ted smiled. "At your service."

Amy smiled in return. The more she chatted with Ted, the more she liked him.

Not good.

She continued. "So, what's number three?"

Ted's face brightened. "The third thing is that, as I mentioned earlier, I've been assigned to be your tour guide during your stay here." He hesitated. "If, that is, you want me to."

Amy felt herself blushing. Part of her wanted so much for Ted to be her tour guide. The other part of her worried about it. If she accepted his offer, she'd be entering precarious territory. First of all, she had to maintain the professionalism required by her position. Second, since Ted had access to the books, he could be a possible suspect in any illegal discovery. Besides, any inappropriate involvement with him would put her in a compromising situation and cast suspicion on her audit. Moreover, she feared getting involved with him on a personal level, a level she'd promised herself never to enter. "Let me think about it."

Ted's gaze flattened. "No problem."

But for some reason, she didn't believe him. Guilt overtook her. Had she hurt him by her response? Should she apologize? Change her mind? Renege on her decision? No. That would be a sign she was failing to maintain a professional attitude and she was weakening in her resolve to keep herself at a distance from all men, including Ted McMasters.

She decided to let the matter drop. "So, my next question is where will I be doing the audit?"

Ted took a sip of his coffee. "We have a small computer room with a computer reserved only for the company ledgers. You'll be able to work quietly in there, free of distractions. I'll give you a key so you can come and go as you please."

Amy took the last sip of her coffee. "That sounds great! I'll probably arrive early and work late. I need to remind myself that I have only three weeks to get this job done."

Ted rose and retrieved a key from his desk. He then handed it to Amy. "Here's your key. Let me take you to the computer room."

Amy placed her empty coffee cup on the table. "Thanks for the great Texas brew. Or should I say, thanks to your mom."

"I'll pass the thanks on to her. She'll enjoy your compliment." Ted hesitated. "Maybe you'll get to meet her someday."

Amy gave him a questioning look. "That would be nice. If I do, I'll tell her what a wonderful son she raised."

This time it was Ted's turn to blush. "Thanks."

Amy followed him out of his office to a small, adjacent room.

Ted unlocked it with his own key and allowed her to enter before him.

The room was the size of a small cubicle. Two cushioned chairs stood behind a table on which sat a large computer screen and a keyboard. A tall window to the right of the computer table allowed for the entrance of outside light. Today a low bank of dark clouds overhead dimmed that light.

"I apologize for the size of the room. I hope you won't feel cramped in here."

"It's fine, really. I prefer the coziness and the quiet. It will help me stay focused."

Ted sat down, turned on the computer, and then patted the seat next to his. "Here. Let me show you how to access the files."

Amy sat down next to Ted while he logged on. "I'll see to it that you get computer access with your own username and password."

"Thanks." Sitting so close to him stirred her senses. She inched away, determined to keep her resolve. Men were off limits, no matter how handsome or witty they were. Underneath all those masculine good looks and charm lurked a heart capable of inflicting pain. And she, for one, would be on guard against it.

A spreadsheet of numbers appeared on the screen. As Ted reached up toward the screen to point out a questionable entry on the spreadsheet, Amy pointed to his wristwatch.

"Nice watch. What kind is it?"

Ted glanced down at his wrist and smiled. "Thanks. It's a smartwatch that tracks different aspects of one's health. It even tracks where I've been and when. And, if I lose it, I have an app on my phone that can locate it."

"No kidding? It actually records your location?"

"Yes. It's amazing. It keeps a log of my day's activities, where I've been, what I've done, and it helps me stay focused and disciplined."

Amy chuckled. "Maybe I should get one of those for myself. I could use a log of how and where I spend my time." She made a mental note of the product name to check it out later. At the end of the audit, she'd treat herself to one as a reward.

Ted pointed to the screen once again. "This is the first entry I discovered that seemed suspicious to me. It's a payment for a line-of-credit loan I can't locate."

"What's the amount?"

"Four hundred eighty-seven dollars a month. And it was paid for several consecutive months for nearly two years." Ted calculated aloud. "That's a total of almost twelve thousand dollars."

"Not a bad chunk of money. What's the line of credit for, and who set it up?"

Ted shook his head. "I have no idea."

Amy made a note of the entry. "This is something we definitely need to explore further. Embezzlers sometimes set up lines of credit without the company's knowledge and then draw on the line of credit for personal purchases. On the books, it simply looks like an LOC payment, when, in reality, it's embezzlement because the line of credit is fraudulent."

Ted arched his brows. "Interesting. I didn't know that."

Amy reached for the mouse to scroll down, not realizing that Ted's hand was still on it. A spark of electricity shot through her as her hand brushed against his before he moved it away. She recoiled and caught her breath. She wouldn't let that happen again. "We need to list and calculate the number and dates of all the line-of-credit payments." In some way, she'd have to find out who made each of the entries.

With the mouse now under her complete control, she kept scrolling. "Another thing. Embezzlers don't use only one means of embezzlement. The culprit here could have used several other means of stealing money from the company."

Ted scratched his head. "Unbelievable! I also discovered several entries for small purchases of office supplies, like notebooks. We don't use notebooks around here. Everything is done on computer."

"That's another red flag. Embezzlers usually steal in small amounts that are not readily noticed."

He turned toward her and smiled. "You sure know a lot about embezzlers."

She laughed. "After I got my accounting degree, I took some graduate courses in fraud detection."

Ted instructed her to continue scrolling down the screen and then stopped her. "Here are a few more for the same item of office supplies. It seems as though the purchase was made every couple of months."

Amy made a note of the entries on her legal pad. "Anything else?"

"Yes, there are several other unusual purchases like these. Interestingly, most of them are for small amounts, under $500."

"As I said, frequent small expenditures for unusual purchases are often a sign of embezzlement. Any auditor worth her salt knows this common trick." She drew in a deep breath. "Is there any way of knowing who made the purchases?"

"Our purchasing department takes care of providing supplies for the office."

"Yes, but who actually enters which receipts here in the ledger? Is there any way of knowing that?"

"Not upfront. The computer automatically records the username and password of the person making the entry. But this information is embedded, so only a computer technician can retrieve the log."

"Can I get a copy of the three usernames and passwords?"

"I'm willing to give you mine, but I'm not sure if Silvia and Giorgio would be willing to give you theirs."

"That could be a problem. Knowing their log-in info would greatly help me in pinning down the culprit."

"I'll ask them."

"No. Let me ask them. They might be more willing to give them to me than to you."

"Good point."

Amy furrowed her brows. "Is there any way you know of that Silvia or Giorgio could have discovered yours?"

"Not unless I told them. And I didn't."

"Are you absolutely sure they could not have discovered yours?"

Ted hesitated. "Well, I can't be absolutely sure, I guess. But we've never shared ours with one another."

"What about you? Did you write yours down anywhere?"

"They're in my cell phone so I can remember them. But no one has access to my cell phone. I always carry it with me."

Amy filed that bit of information in the back of her mind. "Okay. It looks to me as though we have a clear case of embezzlement on our hands. Now the challenge is to find out who is the embezzler."

"But are you absolutely sure this is a case of embezzlement?"

"Well, so far, I can find no other explanation for the loss of funds. Pharmaceutical sales have not diminished. In fact, they've increased. So, the leakage has to be elsewhere."

Ted nodded. "I see."

Amy sighed. "Once this audit is over, I would highly recommend that only one person be assigned to enter the expenditures instead of three. Your current arrangement allows for too many loopholes and not enough accountability."

"I agree."

"But here we are today, and we have to deal with the situation at hand."

"So, where do we start the search for the possible embezzler?"

Amy studied Ted's face.

"You don't think I'm the guilty one, do you?"

"Ted, I have to be objective about this. I can't rule anyone out yet until I make further investigations."

He slowly nodded. "I understand." The look on his face revealed pain.

"Who on your staff holds a company credit card?"

"The same three musketeers: Giorgio, Silvia, and I."

"I'll need to take a look at the credit card statements. I also want to see the statements for your personal credit cards."

"Personal credit cards? What do they have to do with anything?"

"Embezzlers often make purchases on their personal credit cards and then pay them with company funds."

"But how do they do that?"

"They link their personal cards with the company bank account and have the payment wired from the company account to pay off the credit card bill."

"That's pretty clever."

"Yes, very clever—and a crime." The musky smell of Ted's cologne aroused her senses as it rose to her nostrils. "There was a famous embezzlement case a few years back where the principal accounting officer of a headphone-manufacturing corporation did just that. She put large personal purchases on her credit card and then paid them off through wire transfers originating from a company bank account."

Ted turned toward her. "Whoa! What happened to her?"

"She was imprisoned for eleven years. The judge went easy on her because she cooperated and didn't give the court a hard time."

At the sudden touch of fur against her leg, Amy screamed and jumped up.

Ted looked at her in surprise. "What's wrong?"

"Something furry just brushed against my leg."

Ted laughed. "Oh, that's just Callie."

Amy tried to regain her composure. Talk about a lapse in professionalism. "Who's Callie?"

"She's our resident cat." Ted reached down to pick up the feline creature. "Hey, Callie, you scared our visiting auditor. Now, was that a nice thing to do?" He stroked the cat's soft fur and then offered her to Amy. "Amy, meet Callie. Callie, meet Amy."

Amy took the furry creature from Ted and cuddled her against her chest. "Where did you get her?"

"I found her outside the office one day. She seemed lost and forlorn, so I brought her inside."

Ted McMasters was something else. He even cared for stray animals. How many men would do that? "What did Giorgio say?"

"Well, at first he wasn't too keen on having a cat roaming around the office. But after I convinced him that cats pretty much take care of themselves, he agreed. Since then, Callie has become our office mascot."

Amy stroked the lovely creature. "Her coloring is beautiful. And she seems pretty friendly as cats go."

"If you feed her, she'll be your friend for life." Ted reached into his pants pocket and withdrew some cat treats.

"You carry cat treats with you?" Amy's heart melted at Ted's kindness.

He smiled. "Of course! Here you go, Callie." He reached toward the cat who instantly grabbed the treat with her mouth.

The proximity of Ted's hand next to Amy's face sent a chill through her. It was time to get back to work. No more of this nonsense that could derail her from her determined course of action regarding Ted.

She gently handed the cat back to him. "It was nice to meet you, Callie, but I've got work to do. You're a cute cat, but I can't lose my job over you."

And she certainly wasn't about to lose her heart over Ted McMasters, either.

* * * *

Back in his office, Ted stared at the email on his computer screen. It was from Silvia and expressed her concern yet again about the audit. Why, all of a sudden, was Silvia worried about the audit? Before Amy came, Silvia never mentioned the books except at their quarterly meeting.

Ted scratched his head. Maybe there was something more going on here. His discovery of inexplicable entries in the ledger, such as the line of credit, had aroused his suspicions. He'd mentioned those suspicions to Giorgio, but not to Silvia. Giorgio had summarily dismissed them, citing Silvia's consummate organizational skills. No doubt she was well-organized. But well-organized did not necessarily equate to honest.

Ted smelled a rat. All of the questionable entries involved unusual payees. Some related to jewelers, others to vacation resorts and high-end restaurants. One payment of several thousand dollars was made to a Swiss furrier. On occasion, Enson entertained clients at high-end restaurants but never at vacation resorts. Nor did the company purchase jewelry or furs for any client.

Did the embezzler naïvely think such expenditures would not eventually be discovered? Especially with payee names that invited scrutiny?

Ted glanced at the clock. In a few moments, he'd return to the computer room to check on Amy. The thought of his American compatriot and fellow Texan warmed his heart. To his dismay, he found himself wanting to be near her. Wanting to know more about her. Wanting to develop a friendship with her.

His better self stood firmly against anything more than that.

He couldn't allow himself to go there. He couldn't fall into the love trap ever again. And yes, it was a trap. All love was a trap. You gave and gave and then you lost. You laughed and laughed and then you cried. You made yourself vulnerable again and again, only to be rejected once more.

The alarm on his cell phone sounded. Time to feed Callie. He went to the small office kitchen and took the milk carton from the refrigerator. Then he walked to the corner of his office where Callie's ceramic milk bowl sat and filled it to the rim. In a few seconds, Callie appeared and began furiously to lick up the milk. In a few moments, it was gone.

"My, my, Callie! You must have been really hungry."

She meowed and rubbed her fur against his pant leg.

Ted picked her up. "Would you like to pay Amy a visit? I'm sure she'd enjoy seeing you again."

Callie purred.

Ted nuzzled her. "Okay. That settles it. Let's go."

Carrying Callie close to his chest, he made his way to the computer room. His heart pounding, he knocked before opening the door. "Hi! Look who came to visit you."

Amy turned toward him. "Why if it isn't Callie? Hi, Callie!" She reached for the furry cat and took her into her arms. "Don't you look happy!"

"She just had her lunch. A bowlful of milk."

Amy held the cat under the creature's front legs and looked at her. "You must have been really hungry." Then Amy nestled Callie in the crook of her neck and stroked her. The picture of Amy holding the cat engraved itself in Ted's mind. One day, she could be holding a baby in her arms. Their baby. He quickly dismissed the thought. "How's it going?"

Amy smiled. "It's going." She gently placed Callie on the floor.

Ted sat down next to her, his pulse rate quickening.

Amy glanced at him. "I found something that drew my attention big time."

"What's that?"

"A significant expenditure of two thousand dollars to a vacation resort in Greece. Do you know what that was for?"

"I can't imagine. We don't reward clients with vacations, especially not at vacation resorts."

"Well, according to this ledger, you do."

Ted leaned in to get a closer look. In doing so, he accidentally brushed against Amy's arm. Fire rushed through his veins. He pulled back. "I've never heard of this place. Did you check if it really exists?"

"No. But that's a great idea." Amy googled the name of the resort. "You're right. There is no such place."

"Very interesting. So, what do you make of it?"

"Embezzlers sometimes create fictitious payees, pretend to pay them with company funds, but then pocket the funds."

"Do you think that's what happened here?"

"It's looking very probable."

"But who set up the fictitious payee?'

Amy turned toward him. "Well, since only you, Silvia, and Giorgio have access to the books, it has to be one of the three of you." Amy hesitated. "Unless someone else got into the books illegally."

Ted rubbed his forehead. Who could have possibly gotten into the books illegally? And how? "I don't think anyone accessed the books illegally. I think it's either Silvia or Giorgio."

"Or someone else."

His gaze locked onto hers. "Surely you're not including me in the 'someone else,' are you?"

Amy squared her gaze on him. "Ted, it could be anyone. I hope you understand that I have to remain objective in all of this. It's an auditor's role to determine whether embezzlement has actually occurred. But, if, indeed, embezzlement has occurred, it's a country's legal system—in this case, Italy's—to determine the identity of the embezzler. I simply present the facts as I have discovered them." Her eyes were pleading, "I certainly hope you aren't the guilty one, and I personally don't think you are. But I can't make that judgment. It's time to get the police in on this. I've spoken with Mr. Conklin in New York, and he advised me to check with the computer technician to determine if he can identify who made each entry. Mr. Conklin also advised me to call in Italian authorities."

Ted raked his fingers through his hair. "Okay. I have a tennis partner in the police force. I'll call him."

Amy hesitated. "I prefer to contact the police myself and allow them to assign someone of their choice to the case."

Ted drew back, his stomach dropping to his feet. So, Amy didn't really trust him. That hurt. And hurt badly. What could he do to prove to her that he was innocent? Maybe spending an afternoon with him visiting the *Duomo* on a Saturday before she left and going out to dinner would convince her he was an honest guy. "Okay. You're right. You call the final shot." He hesitated. "Hey, on another note, have you thought anymore about my being your tour guide? If you agree, I'd like to take you to the *Duomo* and the *Galleria* one Saturday before you leave, and then to dinner. What do you say?"

Amy bit her lip. "I'm not sure, Ted."

His chest hitched. Swallowing the lump in his throat, he pushed back his chair and got up. "It's all right. I understand where you're coming from. I'd react the same way if I were in your shoes."

She turned toward him, hurt in her eyes. "Ted, please understand. I'm not accusing you. It's just that—"

"Yes. I know. It's just that, until proven otherwise, you have to assume that I could be the embezzler."

She nodded. "My job dictates that I do. I can't draw any conclusions until we have all the facts."

"When you have all the facts, you'll see that I'm not guilty." He lowered his voice. "I may be a lot of bad things, but I'm not dishonest." His eyes met hers. "But I guess I'll have to trust the Lord to defend me."

Amy nodded. "At this point, that's the only thing you can do."

Chapter Six

A fter Ted left, Amy put her head in her hands. She'd hurt him and hurt him badly. The look on his face had spoken volumes.

But why did she even care? He was nothing more to her than a temporary co-worker, one who'd slip out of her life in a few short weeks. After that, she'd return to the States, and that would be the end of Ted.

But would it?

Her stomach churning, she got up and walked to the window. Something was going on inside her. Something she both wanted and feared at the same time. Something that both drew her and repelled her. Ted had sparked something in her soul she didn't want sparked. But the more she tried to stifle the spark, the more it resisted stifling.

If she were truly honest with herself, she'd allowed herself to cross the boundary between professional and personal. She'd entered dangerous territory, territory that could jeopardize her impartiality in the audit and make her motives subject to suspicion. From here on out, she'd have to watch herself. To keep her distance. To suppress her emotions.

Yet, good manners required she accept his kind invitation to visit the *Duomo*, didn't they? After all, she was Enson's guest while in Italy. And Enson's vice-president wanted to treat her as such. To refuse would be rude.

She returned to her desk. She'd send Ted a text message and tell him she'd be happy to spend one Saturday afternoon visiting the *Duomo* and the *Galleria*. By accepting his invitation, she'd show him she had no ill feelings toward him, despite the fact that she needed to remain objective in the investigation. Then, afterwards, she'd do her best to finish the audit ahead of schedule and return to New York early. Once out of sight, Ted would be out of mind.

After Amy finished the text message, she hit SEND. An unexpected thrill ran through her. The thought of spending an entire afternoon with Ted outside of the work environment ignited something within her that had remained dormant ever since her father left. That something was hope.

For the first time in a long time, hope rose big within her. Hope that her life could have meaning beyond numbers. Hope that maybe, just maybe, one day she could trust again.

But was she taking an unnecessary chance?

A knock on the computer room door caught Amy's attention. She looked up.

Ted walked in, a smile on his face, and sat down next to her. "Callie got your text about Saturday. And has been meowing ever since."

Amy burst into laughter.

Ted grinned. "I'm glad you changed your mind."

"So am I." The quiver in her voice betrayed the quiver in her heart.

"I'd hate to have you be in Milan and not visit the *Duomo*. That would be sacrilegious."

She smiled. "I think it'll do me good mentally, too. I'm about to go stir crazy if I look at any more numbers."

"All work and no play make Jack a dull boy."

"And Amy a dull girl."

He gave her a look that made her heart race. "You'll never be dull."

"Nor will you." The words slipped out of her heart.

Something clicked between them.

Ted rose to leave. "We'll set up a time on a Saturday before you leave to go to the *Galleria* and then to the *Duomo*. Then I'll take you to one of Milan's best restaurants, *La Porta Rossa*. I think you'll love it."

"I'm sure I will."

"I'm leaving now so you can work ahead. I don't want any last-minute cancellation for our outing because I kept you from your work."

She wanted to tell him he could keep her from her work anytime. Instead, she teased him. "Yes. It would be awful if I missed the *Duomo* because of you."

"Agreed!" He smiled, his eyes revealing a look that both frightened her and delighted her.

After Ted left, she took a deep breath, promising herself she'd never fall in love with Ted McMasters.

But why, deep down inside, did she believe she already had?

* * * *

Arms folded tightly across her chest, Silvia nervously paced Giorgio's office floor, vitriol pouring out of her mouth. "That woman is nothing but trouble. I wish she'd never come. She asked for my username and password to the ledger."

"She asked me for mine, too."

Silvia's eyes widened. "Did you give them to her?"

"Of course not."

"I refused to give her mine as well." Silvia sat down in a chair across from Giorgio. "Already she's created animosity between Ted and us." She was careful to include Giorgio, afraid to imply that the animosity was only between Ted and her. She couldn't risk antagonizing Giorgio at the moment. Thankfully, he would be too thick to see it for what it really was.

She pointed a warning index finger at him. "Mark my words, Giorgio, if you don't get rid of Amy Torelli, she will be the end of us. If she discovers what we've been doing with the books, we'll both end up in prison."

Giorgio lifted his palms in surrender. "What do you want me to do? I can't send her back to New York. You know as well as I do that we're under the jurisdiction of headquarters and must do what they say. I can't just fire her."

Silvia was on top of him. "But you can find something wrong and then complain about it to the New York office. Surely, they'll call her back and send someone else instead." Someone less attractive, who wasn't a threat to her. Someone in whom Ted would have no interest.

Silvia sighed, unwilling openly to acknowledge the truth that smarted at the core of her being. Amy was gorgeous, and Ted, plain and simple, was falling for her.

And Silvia hated that fact. Hated it with every fiber of her being.

Giorgio lowered his feet from his desk and planted them on the floor. "Silvia, you are being ridiculous. I can't just make up a problem with Miss Torelli. I must have proof. Undeniable proof. Otherwise, my own job will be jeopardized." He gave her a probing look. "Frankly, I think there's more to your anger than meets the eye." He smiled knowingly. "Perhaps you're worried about a little competition in the beauty area?" His words mingled joking with sarcasm.

Silvia's blood rose to boiling. "You scoundrel! How dare you say such a thing?"

He rose from his desk and came toward her, taking her into his arms. "Silvia, there is no woman more beautiful than you." He moved his lips toward hers, but she turned her face away. "This is not the right time, Giorgio. Can't you see I'm upset?"

"Yes. And you're even more beautiful to me when you're upset."

She pushed him away. "Nothing you say can assuage my

anger."

He threw up his hands in disgust. "Then live with it!" Obviously exasperated, he returned to his desk chair and put his feet on top of his desk once again. "When you get over your anger, come back and I'll show you that you don't need a man like Ted when you have me."

Silvia's heart lurched. Giorgio's stunning comment took her off her guard and sent her reeling. To her great surprise, he was more perceptive than she'd given him credit for. Part of her liked that, and part of her worried about it. She'd have to be more careful in her behavior not only toward Amy but also toward Ted. Most of all, she'd have to keep her mouth shut about her feelings toward both. If Giorgio got the wrong impression, she could lose both him and Ted.

And then where would she be?

Besides, she couldn't risk Giorgio's turning on her regarding the funds they'd been stealing from the company. Funds he knew about but had turned a blind eye toward so as to compensate her for her favors over the years. So far, they'd managed to get away with their thievery under the guise of company expenses. But now that Amy was here, would their paper house come crumbling down? Would she and Giorgio end up in prison?

Silvia shuddered at the prospect.

She approached Giorgio and caressed his face from behind him. "I'm sorry." She leaned toward him and purred into his ear. "You're the only man for me. As long as you find me beautiful, it doesn't matter how beautiful any other woman is."

Ten years with Giorgio had helped her perfect her lying skills. Truth was, it did matter that Amy Torelli was beautiful. It mattered a great deal. Not because of Giorgio but because of Ted.

Was Giorgio also astute enough to realize he'd become a has-been to her? A man in whom she no longer had any interest? A man whose prime had come and gone, and whose career was fast coming to a close? Soon he would no longer do her any good. No longer be of benefit to her.

No longer demand her time and attention.

No. She needed new pastures. Fresher pastures. Livelier pastures.

And she'd found them in Ted.

Unless Amy stole him from her.

Silvia had grown tired of the old. She wanted and needed the new.

She came to Giorgio's side. "You know I will always love you, don't you, *tesoro*? My treasure?"

He grabbed her by the arm. "You take me for an old fool, don't you, Silvia?"

Her muscles tensed as heat rose to her cheeks. "What do you mean?"

His gaze locked onto hers. "You know exactly what I mean. I haven't lived nearly sixty years not to be able to recognize when a woman desires me and when she doesn't."

Silvia averted her eyes. "I don't understand."

A scowl crossed his face. "I think you do."

She swallowed hard. He'd caught her red-handed. What should she do now? What *could* she do? "I don't know what you're talking about."

He drew her closer. "Silvia, I've known you for ten years. They've been wonderful years. For me, at least. But I can tell you're growing tired of me."

She lowered her eyes.

He insisted. "You are, aren't you?"

She wanted to run. To hide. To dig a hole and jump in. "Let's say, I've grown accustomed to you, Giorgio. You're like an old shoe. Comfortable and safe."

"Let's not sugar-coat it. Tell me the truth. You no longer love me. Instead, you have your eye on Ted McMasters, right?" He sighed. "I'm beginning to wonder if you ever did love me for me, or for what I could give you."

A tremor of guilt rippled through her heart. Giorgio had her on the spot. And no matter how much she tried, there was no getting off of it.

"I do find him—" She hesitated, searching for the safest word. "Interesting."

"Aha! Now you've confessed the truth." Giorgio tugged on her arm. "But only interesting?"

Could she admit she found Ted far more than interesting? That she found him fascinating? Attractive? Desirable?

Desirable enough to marry?

She couched her words in another lie. "Perhaps slightly more than interesting."

Giorgio grew quiet. "Then my suspicions have been well founded." His voice was almost a whisper.

A pang of pity shot through Silvia's chest and lodged in her throat. "Giorgio, I owe you my very life."

He slowly rose and waved a dismissive hand at her. "You owe me nothing, Silvia. On the contrary, it is I who owe you everything." He lowered his voice to an anguished whisper. "Everything." He moved away.

She followed him with her eyes as he walked toward the window. His back turned toward her, he looked like only a shadow of the man she'd served for the past decade. Time and stress had taken their toll on him. His stance reflected brokenness, hopelessness, and defeat.

She approached him from behind and placed her arms around his waist.

He did not move.

She leaned her head against his back, more from pity than from anything else.

"Silvia, it's over between us." The words sounded hollow.

She raised her head. "What do you mean?"

"I mean exactly what I said. It's over between us."

She could not bring herself to protest. Backing away, she turned and left the room. For the first time in her relationship with Giorgio, she accepted the truth.

But with the truth would come its consequences.

* * * *

Ted sat at his desk, mindlessly poring over the sales reports for the last quarter. It fell to him as vice-president to review the quarterly reports, compare them to the last quarter, and then send a report to Giorgio. So far, this quarter's sales report showed a significant drop in profits.

Again.

Ted released a sharp sigh. Once again, he felt disillusioned with his job. Was this what life was all about? Reviewing quota reports, pushing hard to increase profits, only to do the same thing the next quarter, and the next? What good was he doing for humanity? Nothing. Sure, the pharmaceuticals Enson manufactured helped sick people, but Ted never saw those people. Never had any kind of human contact with them. And, for all he knew, those medications weren't always reaching the people they were meant to reach.

He stared at the computer screen in front of him. The numbers blurred as Amy's face emerged over them. He quickly dismissed it. Her presence in the Italian office troubled him in a way he hadn't expected. She'd broken every stereotypical image he'd had of an auditor, sending his heart reeling. She was a clear and present emotional danger, a potential trap into which he vowed he would not allow himself to fall.

Shaking off his inner turmoil, he rose from his chair and walked to the window. The afternoon sun had already reached the halfway mark on its descent toward the horizon. In a few short hours, dusk would settle over the city, and he'd finish another day on the job.

A day like every other day.

He stuffed his fists into his pockets. Why was he here anyway? Was it because God had sent him here, or because he was running away from something? As he looked back, he'd been running for a long time. At least, it felt that way.

First, he'd run from a dad who was disappointed in a son who had not met his outlandish expectations.

That memory stung and stung deeply.

Then he'd run from the pain of the broken relationship with Shawna, who hadn't been able to bear his insecurities and had ditched him for a more stable guy.

Another sting.

Now he was running from Amy, for fear of botching it up yet again. He closed his eyes. Didn't he know how to do anything else but run?

And you're running from Me, too, son.

The Lord's still, small voice caught Ted off guard. He hadn't considered that he'd been running from the Lord. "How so, Lord?"

I called you to be a pastor.

If one's soul could blush from guilt, Ted's soul now blushed deeply. "Yes, you did, Lord."

My calling is irrevocable, son.

Ted remembered the Scripture verse in Romans 11: 29. He remembered the very day he'd gone forward at the altar in the little church in that tiny Texas town to accept Jesus as his personal Savior and Lord. He remembered the same still, small voice that had said to him back then, *Feed My sheep.*

Yet, despite all of his good intentions, he'd forgotten about the voice. He'd pushed it aside when the lure of being somebody drew him away. All of his life, he'd wanted to be somebody. To be recognized as having worth. To leave his mark on the world.

So, when the opportunity to climb the corporate ladder with Enson came his way, he'd grabbed it. Now he'd show the world who Ted McMasters really was. Now he'd pay his dad back for the bitter humiliation he'd put his son through.

Now, he'd prove to himself that he could make it in spite of his dad's rejection.

"A penny for your thoughts." Silvia's voice broke through his pondering.

Ted turned suddenly. "My thoughts cost more than a penny."

She sidled up to him. "I'm willing to pay any price."

Ted seethed. This wasn't the first time Silvia had hit on him. And the hits had grown more frequent. This last one was the straw that broke the camel's back. The woman was evil. Just plain evil. He turned on her, fire raging in his belly. "Get out of here! I've had enough of your wicked wiles. How brazen can you be, not only harassing me, but also harassing me here at work? Have you no shame? No self-respect? Obviously, not!"

Ted walked away from her. "You have no chance whatsoever with me, Silvia. None! So, stop trying! If you think you're the kind of woman I want, you're wrong. Absolutely wrong!" His body shook as he walked toward his computer.

"Very well." Her voice was resolute. "If that's what you want, that's what you'll get."

"Good!"

"But know this, Mr. Vice-President, no one messes with Silvia Villano and gets away with it." With that, she stalked out of his office, slamming the door behind her.

Ted sat down at his computer desk, still shaking. His stomach roiled with acid. That woman would be the death of him if he'd let her. He should have kicked her out long ago.

But he'd been afraid of losing his job. Silvia was too close to

Giorgio Bassetti for comfort. For Ted's comfort. Over the past year, Ted had discovered that Giorgio was just a puppet in the sly hands of his personal assistant. She manipulated him with finesse, and he seemed totally oblivious to her manipulation. It was she who ran Enson Italia, and she ran it to her advantage. Giorgio was too much of a wimp to stop her.

In a way, Ted felt sorry for him. He was a broken man whose adulterous behavior had resulted in a messy divorce, setting his life on a downward spiral from which he'd never recovered. A man who'd heeded the world's ways and gotten the world's consequences. But that had been his choice.

Ted had a sudden desire to resign. To leave it all and go back to Texas to pastor a little church in a tiny town.

What he should have done in the first place.

Just then, Amy knocked on his office door and walked in. "I thought I'd find you here."

He swiveled in his chair, his heart skipping a beat. "What's up?"

"I think I've found something big."

He got up and followed her to the computer room.

Amy sat down at the computer, and Ted took the chair beside her.

She pointed to the screen. "Do you see this purchase for $3,478?"

He looked closely. "Yes."

"Notice the payee. RobMan Enterprises. I googled the name of the organization and its owner. It's headed up by a man named Roberto Manero."

Ted's heart froze. He turned to Amy. "Roberto Manero is a big Mafia boss here in Italy."

Amy's eyes widened. "Wow! That puts a whole new slant on things."

Ted nodded. "The plot thickens, doesn't it?"

Amy pointed to the screen. "Even worse than that, I found seven payments made to the same company. But why? What would the embezzler gain from paying a Mafioso?"

Ted looked at her "A great deal. For one thing, protection. The Mafia protects its own unless one turns on them." He continued. "For another thing, the Mafia could have established a deal with the embezzler to syphon profits from Enson in exchange for some nice perks."

Amy nodded. "But your income base seems to be intact. It doesn't look as though Enson Italia has lost money in sales. It could be that your sales figures have been padded."

Ted's head spun. How much worse could the situation get?

Amy sighed. "My guess is that the embezzler is involved with RobMan Enterprises and that RobMan is a Mafia front company receiving Enson funds under the guise of a legitimate service. The embezzler could really be paying Manero in exchange for perks and promises."

"What kind of promises?"

"Promises of lifelong financial security. Promises of protection for family members. Promises of protection from the cops."

Ted released a low whistle. "So, what do we do now?"

"Since this case now seems to reach beyond the borders of Italy, I think it's time to involve Interpol. I've gotten to the point where we need international law enforcement to do the investigations. This is beyond my scope of expertise."

Ted raked his fingers through his hair. "It's beyond mine as well."

"I'm also going to call Mr. Conklin to tell him about this latest discovery." Amy's look was intense. "Meanwhile, I suggest you keep it to yourself. If anyone finds out, things could get really bad really fast."

Ted nodded. As if things weren't already bad enough.

Chapter Seven

Seething with rage, Silvia sped along the highway in her red Lamborghini on her way to Giorgio's country estate outside the perimeters of Milan. How dare Ted humiliate her by refusing her advances? No man had ever refused her advances.

Ted would pay for this, and pay big time. Not only would she see to it that he lost his job, but she'd also make sure that she destroyed him for life.

Anything to show Ted McMasters that he didn't mess with Silvia Villano and get away with it.

Anything to keep him and Amy Torelli from getting together.

Jealousy dug its vicious talons into Silvia's soul, squeezing the very lifeblood out of her heart. She swerved, just missing a pedestrian walking along the highway.

Uttering a curse, she pressed her foot even harder on the accelerator, enjoying the sense of power the speed of the vehicle gave her. She'd devise a plan to destroy Ted's reputation completely. To the point he'd never again be able to find a job or build a career.

And she would use sweet Amy Torelli to do it.

Silvia laughed aloud, her red hair blowing in the wind.

Yes, sweet Amy Torelli. Silvia wasn't so stupid as not to have noticed the look in Amy's eyes when Ted was in the room. No question Amy was in love with him. Even a fool would have noticed it.

And no question Ted was in love with Amy.

The very thought of the two of them together gnawed at Silvia's insides.

She smiled as a sinister plot took shape in her mind. What if Amy discovered that Ted McMasters, the man she loved, had been embezzling money from Enson Italia? What would that do to Amy's love for him? And how would she report the embezzlement to the higher-ups? Would she report it? If she didn't, she'd lose her own job. If she did, she'd lose the man she loved. What a nice and neat predicament for the young auditor from New York! No amount of brains or beauty would get her out of that one.

The more Silvia thought about it, the more she savored her plan. The best part was that she already had the right method in place to execute it, and to execute it without any evidence of her participation in it. Not even Giorgio would have a clue that she was involved. Ted McMasters wouldn't know what hit him.

And Amy Torelli would wish she had never come to Milan.

* * * *

As soon as Ted left, Amy brought up Mr. Conklin's number in her cell phone. She tapped on the number and waited.

"Wendell Conklin here." Mr. Conklin's gruff voice sent a wave of relief flooding through her.

"Hello, Mr. Conklin. This is Amy."

"Well, hello, Amy. Something big must have happened for you to call me."

She appreciated the way he immediately got to the bottom line. "Actually, yes. Quite big. In fact, bigger than I'd expected."

"Go ahead."

"It looks as though not only is Enson Italia involved in embezzlement, but embezzlement connected to the Mafia."

Mr. Conklin remained silent for a brief moment. "Well, this is bad news. Bad news, indeed. Have you called the police yet?"

"Actually, I've contacted Interpol. There are signs of international implications since some of the entries were paid to vendors outside of Italy."

"I see." Mr. Conklin cleared his throat. "Any clues yet as to the culprits?"

"Not yet. I'm still waiting for the computer technician to retrieve the embedded identifications. But I have my hunches, although I'm not ready to confirm anything just yet. It's not my job to accuse, only to expose."

"Yes. That's right. We'll leave the accusations to the police who will evaluate all the evidence."

"That's what I plan to do."

"Good. Meanwhile, keep your eyes open. We may have to clean house pretty soon."

"I think so, too."

He hesitated. "Amy, are you safe?" Mr. Conklin's voice sounded concerned.

"As safe as can be."

"Stay close to Ted. He's a good guy."

"I'll take your word for it, Mr. Conklin. He seems like a good guy to me, too, but I can't rule out anyone. He, Silvia, and Giorgio are the only ones who have access to the ledger, as far as I can tell."

"I hear you. But, nonetheless, my gut tells me you can trust Ted."

"Thanks, Mr. Conklin." She didn't want to add that she was a big girl and could take care of herself. Mr. Conklin was old school. Truth be told, old school felt good right about now.

"Keep in close touch. I'll do some investigating from my end here in New York so we can coordinate our efforts."

"That would be helpful."

"Thanks for the update, Amy."

"You're welcome, sir."

"Stay safe."

"I will, sir."

Amy ended the call and got up from the computer table to

stretch. She was already two weeks into the audit, and things were looking worse than she'd anticipated. A shiver ran through her. Since the embezzlement involved the Mafia, she could be in grave danger.

She dismissed the thought. She'd head over to Ted's office to fill him in on her conversation with Mr. Conklin. Talking to Ted always made her feel good. And right about now, she certainly needed to feel good about something.

She found Ted seated behind his desk with Callie on his lap. Amy laughed. "You and that cat! What are you going to do when you become company president and move to the New York office?"

He laughed at her teasing. "I'm going to take Callie with me. And she'll sit on my lap in the Manhattan office just as she's sitting on my lap now."

Amy raised an eyebrow.

"But, there will be a big difference."

She settled in the chair in front of Ted's desk and crossed her legs. "What's that?"

"She'll be wearing a collar with the inscription, 'Callie the Cat: VP of the New York Branch'."

Amy laughed. "You wouldn't dare."

Ted gave her his brilliant smile. "I would so dare."

There it was again. That quick repartee. That spark between them. That connection that flowed swift and free. As though they were of one mind and one heart.

Amy swallowed hard. Because they were.

Ted changed the subject. "You must be exhausted. How about we spend this coming Saturday afternoon at the *Duomo*? I've been assigned to be your personal escort, remember?"

She tilted her head. "Who assigned you?"

He gave her a sheepish look. "I'm sworn to secrecy."

"By whom?"

"By me."

Amy tried unsuccessfully to suppress a laugh. "Hmm. I see."

"Well, what do you think?"

"I think I should make sure I'm under company authority in visiting the *Duomo* with you. If not, my audit could come under question, and we could open ourselves up to serious accusations. But as long as Giorgio has initiated the visit to the Duomo, we're okay. "

Ted leaned forward and folded his hands on his desk. A smile played around his lips. "Miss Torelli, I assure you that you are under company authority. This visit to the *Duomo* and the *Galleria* is purely courtesy of Enson Italia. And the dinner at *La Porta Rossa* is as well." He smiled. "Actually, we take most of our foreign clients to the *Duomo* and to dinner at *La Porta Rossa*."

"In that case, I accept."

"Excellent. I'll pick you up on Saturday at eleven."

"I'll be ready."

As Amy left Ted's office, one question bombarded her mind: Would she ever be ready to deal with her growing feelings about Ted McMasters?

* * * *

When Silvia reached Giorgio's country estate, she found Roberto Manero and a few of his aides waiting for her. Giorgio had suggested she meet them there since it was not under police radar.

The day was warm and sunny, and a gentle breeze swept across the cypress trees that lined the perimeter of the magnificent estate. A bank of purple wisteria graced the front lawn, along the curb.

Roberto approached her as she pulled up in the circular

driveway in front of the main house. "Why did you need to meet with me so urgently?" He didn't even say hello to her.

She got out of the Lamborghini and slammed the door behind her. "Big problem. I overheard your name come up in a conversation between our vice-president and the auditor from New York."

Roberto raised an eyebrow. "How did you manage that?"

"I eavesdropped at the computer room door." She smiled. "Ted, our vice-president, has been working closely with Amy Torelli, the auditor, and they have seemingly grown quite fond of each other."

Roberto arched his eyebrows? "Really?"

"She's discovered some information that will put us all in the slammer unless we do something fast."

"What kind of information?"

"Suspicious entries paid to you. The money we've been funneling to you from corporate profits in exchange for your services."

Roberto grew pensive but did not respond.

Silvia continued. "Something has to be done to prevent the truth from getting out."

"And how do you propose to do that?"

Silvia lifted her chin. "You're the expert. But I have a plan I want to run by you."

He broke into a sly smile. "You've come to the right place."

Silvia reached into her purse for the key to the house. "Let's go inside where we can sit down and talk."

She led the way up the few steps to the front door and unlocked it. Upon entering, a musty smell filled her nostrils. She proceeded to open some of the casement windows.

The men followed her into a spacious living room. Two large sofas, each one flanked by a Queen Anne chair, lined two of the walls. Silvia took the chair closest to one of the open windows.

Roberto sat on the sofa opposite her, and his two aides took the remaining chairs.

Roberto spoke first. "So, tell me what's been going on."

"As best as I can gather, Amy has discovered several instances of embezzlement. This morning, as I mentioned, I overheard your name come up."

"In what context?"

"When I set up the transfer of Enson Italia's profits to you, I used your legal business name. It was the simplest way for me to identify you while avoiding suspicion."

"Well, I am, after all—let's say—well-known in certain circles." He gave her a wry smile.

Silvia gave him a sidelong glance. "Which is what I think happened. Amy probably investigated RobMan Enterprises and discovered it was owned by you."

Roberto gave her a slow nod. "I see." He glanced at one of his aides. "Miss Torelli is quite an intelligent young woman to make the connection."

Silvia tensed at his compliment of Amy. She leaned forward, her hands clasped tightly on her lap. "I have a plan and want to know what you think."

"What's your plan? Whatever it is, I think we need to act quickly. Amy may have already notified the authorities."

Silvia's muscles tightened. "My plan is to shift the blame to our Vice-President, Ted McMasters."

"How will you do that?"

"I got his username and password from his cell phone."

Roberto raised an eyebrow and smiled approvingly. "We could use you in the Mafia."

Silvia smiled in return. "I plan to log on to the ledger under Ted's name and make it appear as though all the fraudulent entries were made by him." Stealing Ted's username and password from his cell phone had been a great move on her part. She'd pilfered

the information from his phone recently when Ted absent-
mindedly left his phone on his desk while he stepped into the next
room to retrieve some records she'd requested for Giorgio. One
day, when they were talking about the challenges of remembering
login information, Ted had flippantly mentioned that he'd stored
his in his phone.

Roberto steeled his look on her. "Then we'll see if Miss Torelli
is eager enough to report her new boyfriend to the police."

Silvia nodded. "Yes. Then we'll see."

Chapter Eight

On Friday night, after everyone had gone home, Silvia went to the computer room. Looking around her to make sure she was alone, she gingerly turned the key in the lock and entered. The office building had closed for the weekend, and the cleaning crew was making its rounds on the upper floors.

She turned on the tall floor lamp next to the computer and sat down at the table. Her hands trembled as she turned on the machine. She logged on, using Ted's username and password, and pulled up the ledger files. She found the fraudulent entries and would adjust them to reflect that Ted had made the entries. Her actions would remove her from any suspicious connection with the embezzlement and would, instead, implicate Ted.

Silvia smirked at the thought.

One by one, she deleted and then re-entered the original date for every fraudulent entry to make it appear as though Ted had made the entry. Her heart raced as she hurried to complete the task. The cleaning crew usually cleaned the building in descending fashion, from the top floor down. Soon they'd reach the second floor where she was, and she didn't want them finding her there.

She hadn't figured on so many fraudulent entries. The number of them filled her with guilt, a guilt she pushed aside as she'd done so often in the past.

The sound of a vacuum cleaner outside the computer room door startled her. If the cleaning people entered the computer room, she'd have to give them some excuse. What if she locked the door from the inside? No. That wouldn't work. They probably had a key.

Taking a deep breath, she decided to face them head-on. She

got up from the computer. Raising her head high, she opened the door.

A short, middle-aged man pushed a large vacuum cleaner in the hallway. Upon seeing her, he looked up. "*Buona sera, signorina.*"

Silvia gave him a nod. "Could you be a little more quiet with that vacuum cleaner, please?"

The man looked flustered. "*Sì. Sì, signorina.* I'm sorry for disturbing you. I will do the computer room later."

"Thank you." She re-entered the computer room and shut the door behind her. Perhaps she'd made a mistake in showing herself. On the other hand, greeting the man might give him the impression she had nothing to hide.

As she sat back down at the computer table, her heart convicted her.

She had everything to hide. And then some.

* * * *

Amy glanced at the digital clock on the end table next to the bed at her hotel. The display showed one-twelve a.m. She'd been lying in bed for two solid hours, unable to fall asleep. Ted's invitation had troubled her and left her wondering about his motive. Was it truly the gesture of a company vice-president showing his foreign visitor around town? Or was there more to his invitation? A personal element that had nothing to do with Enson Italia?

Why did she hope the latter?

She gave herself a mental slap. She couldn't go there. She must not go there. It was too dangerous. For more reasons than one. First and foremost, she was here on a professional assignment and had to avoid all semblance of impropriety.

Second, she'd promised herself to avoid a romantic relationship, not only with Ted, but also with any man, for that matter.

But her heart pulled her in both directions.

Maybe it was time to call Sara. Amy looked at the clock again. It was now 1:15 a.m. It was 7:15 p.m. in New York. She picked up her cell phone and tapped Sara's number.

"Hey, girlfriend!" Sara's cheery voice was like a warm blanket over Amy's troubled heart. "It's so good to hear from you. I was afraid you'd gone off and married an Italian guy, and I'd never see you again."

Amy laughed. "Oh, come on, Sara. You know me better than that."

"I do know you. That's what worries me." Sara sighed. "So, what's up?"

"Well, I must admit, you're on the right track."

"What do you mean?"

"I mean I did meet a guy, but he's not Italian. He's American and from Texas. He's Enson's vice-president here in Milan."

"Well, that's great. At least, there's a chance that, if you marry him, you might move back to the States one day."

Amy laughed and then grew serious. "I really like him, Sara, but I'm scared."

"Of what?"

"Of breaking my promise never to get involved with a man."

"I told you once before, you're not afraid of men, you're afraid of hurt."

"Okay, I never want to get hurt again."

"Well, that's unrealistic."

"How so?"

"Life is full of hurt. To love is to risk hurt."

Amy pondered Sara's words. Her friend was right.

Sara continued. "Just think of Jesus. He knew the outcome

ahead of time. He knew He'd be rejected and betrayed and maligned and crucified. Yet, He loved us anyway."

Amy considered what Sara said.

"So, tell me about this guy."

Amy proceeded to fill Sara in on Ted and on his invitation to the *Duomo*. "I couldn't decide whether or not to go with him."

"I hope you agreed."

"I did."

"Good. Now put the whole thing in God's hands."

Yes. That was what Amy should have done from the beginning. Mama always said that God had a plan for her life, but that Amy had to cooperate with it. Maybe she should get back to her relationship with the Lord.

"How are things at the New York office?"

"Crazy as usual. We miss you a lot."

"I'll be back soon."

After a few more moments, her conversation with Sara ended. Releasing a sigh of exhaustion, Amy sat up in bed, fluffed her pillow, and plopped down onto it again. Her growing obsession with Ted was causing her undue distraction. Truth was, the more she worked with him, the more she respected and admired him. He was a class act. A man of integrity. A born leader. He had the unique ability to merge courage with compassion. She'd even had this odd, fleeting thought he'd make a great pastor.

But she needed to get a grip and stay focused on the task at hand: the audit. She forced herself to shift focus. Her recent discovery of the Mafia connection behind RobMan Enterprises had rocked her. This was a huge find, and one that could be the key to a major international embezzlement scheme.

But who was the culprit? She hoped it wasn't Ted. He didn't seem like the type capable of stealing. Yet, were her feelings toward him clouding her judgment? Sometimes those who looked the most innocent were the guilty ones.

She turned onto her side and closed her eyes. The thought that Ted could be guilty of any crime ate at her insides. In her mind, he was innocent until proven guilty, as well he should be, and as justice dictated.

And proving Ted guilty was not something she wanted to do anytime this side of eternity.

* * * *

The prospect of entertaining Amy Torelli for an entire Saturday afternoon thrilled Ted beyond measure. On the day of the big occasion, he rose early, more from anticipation than from sufficient rest. He was too excited to eat breakfast. Instead, he poured himself a cup of his mom's Texas brew and sat down to read his Bible.

Early mornings were his favorite time of day. He needed those moments to connect with his Lord. To regroup. To get directions for the day.

And today was no exception. He needed God to tell him what to do about Amy. Ted's heart had grown immensely fond of her. So fond that he felt sure he'd fallen in love with her. At the same time, he feared moving forward. What if Amy rejected him the same way Shawna had? What if Amy discovered that, deep down inside, he was a loser, just as his dad had pegged him.

Was Ted willing to risk another round of rejection for a relationship with Amy?

Perhaps today he'd get his answer.

"Lord, show me Your will." He opened his Bible to Psalm 32. His eyes fell on verse 8: *"I will instruct thee and teach thee in the way which thou shalt go."* The words jumped off the page and leapt into his heart. Yes, God would give him His answer about Amy. And about every other situation he would face in life. God would make a way where there seemed to be no way.

The thought of leaving it all to become a pastor crossed his mind again. He allowed himself free reign to imagine. He saw himself living in a small town in west Texas and pastoring a tiny church in that town. A woman stood at his side. She was lovely and kind and intelligent. As he continued to imagine, he saw that the woman was Amy Torelli.

He swallowed hard. "Lord, are You trying to tell me something about Amy? If so, please make it clear to me." Ted bowed his head and whispered. "Please make it clear."

Chapter Nine

Amy looked through her meager wardrobe in the hotel closet for an outfit to wear to the *Duomo* that afternoon. She'd brought as few items of clothing as possible for her stay in Italy. She'd learned that less is often more in life, especially when one travels.

A hot pink blouse caught her eye. She withdrew it from the closet and placed it against a pair of black slacks lying on the bed. Perfect. She smiled. And not only perfect, but perfectly comfortable.

Ted would be picking her up in two hours. She'd need that long to shower, dress, and put on her makeup. Truth be told, she'd need that long to look her best for him.

The thought of spending the afternoon with Ted sent shivers down her spine. Ever since their playful repartee over which one of them would become president of Enson International, the atmosphere had shifted between them. Not in the wrong direction of jealous competition, but in the right direction of mutual cooperation. Amy had gotten the impression that, despite their common goal of becoming president, neither one of them really wanted the job. But both of them really wanted something else. Something more. Something deeper. Something permanent.

But exactly what that "something" was escaped her. All of her life she'd searched for it. But she hadn't found it yet. Otherwise, why did she still feel a constant sense of dissatisfaction, as though something were missing from her life? Why did she still feel the need to do more? To have more? To be more? What was it she was really looking for?

Maybe she'd discover it today, while spending time with Ted.

After a quick cup of coffee, she showered, wrapped herself in her robe, and then put on her makeup. She wasn't one for wearing much makeup, only just enough to make her coloring look natural. After applying foundation, blush, and mascara, she brushed her long, dark brown tresses and lifted them into a charming ponytail. She wanted to be as comfortable as possible without having to worry about her hair drooping in the heat. Finally, she donned the black slacks and the hot pink blouse. It brought out the sparkle in her hazel eyes.

She stood approvingly in front of the mirror. She looked good and hoped Ted would think so, too.

Amy glanced at the time on her cell phone. Ten-fifty-two. Her heart skipped a beat. Ted would be arriving in a few moments.

Suddenly she had misgivings. Was their visit to the *Duomo* considered a date? Or just a company courtesy? Did Ted really do this kind of thing for all visitors from headquarters? Did Giorgio really know about it? What would Silvia do if she found out? Amy's stomach roiled at this last thought. The woman would skewer her, that's what she'd do.

Amy glanced at her cell phone again. Time to go down to the lobby where Ted would be waiting for her.

She grabbed her room key, a sweater, and her shoulder bag and closed the door behind her. The elevator was just around the corner from her room. She pushed the down button. In a few moments, the elevator door opened and she entered. Several other people were riding down as well. Amy pushed the lobby button and smiled at the others.

In a few seconds, the elevator door opened onto the lobby. Upon exiting, she found Ted right in front of the elevators. "Hi!" She gave him a warm smile.

"Hey!" His eyes widened at the sight of her.

A chill ran through her.

"You look fantastic! A bit different from your office attire, I'd say." He scanned the length of her admiringly.

"You look a bit different yourself without your suit and tie."

His blue-gray cotton polo shirt brought out the blue in the depth of his eyes.

Ted smiled. "Well, are you ready for the tour of your life?"

"The tour of my life?"

"I think you'll agree once you see the inside of the *Duomo* and then climb up to the spires."

"Are you serious? We're going to climb up to the spires?"

"It's the best part. From there you can see the entire city of Milan."

Amy was glad she'd chosen good walking shoes. "Then let's get going."

Ted took her by the elbow and led her outside the hotel to his Fiat. He'd parked it only a few short paces from the hotel entrance. "First stop, the *Galleria*. You'll love the shops and the cosmopolitan atmosphere. It's a main tourist attraction here in Milan. We'll see people from all over the world. Then a quick lunch. Then the *Duomo*. We'll spend a couple of hours there, touring the inside and then climbing up to the spires. The view from the top is amazing."

He opened the passenger-side door and held it while Amy got in.

She was getting used to Ted's tiny Italian car. Although it looked like a toy, it was comfortable and could easily get in and out of tight places. And there were many tight places in Milan.

Ted entered the driver's side and turned on the ignition. "God certainly blessed us with a beautiful day for an outing."

Amy smiled. "Yes." She looked out the passenger window. Ted spoke so naturally of God. Why couldn't she? Ever since Daddy left, she'd turned her back on God. What kind of God would take her father from her? Not any God she wanted to serve. "I can't believe how blue the sky is here in Italy."

"Not as blue as the Texas sky."

She turned toward him. "You really miss Texas, don't you?"

"More than I'd realized. I think having you here reminds me of our home state."

"But I haven't lived in Texas for eighteen years."

"You still have that Texas look. That Texas charm. That—." He struggled to find the right word. "That Texas heart." He turned toward her and smiled. "It's something I don't think you ever lose."

Amy looked at him. "Thank you." She hesitated. "You know, it's really kind of you to show me around."

"Hey! It's the least I can do, especially for a fellow Texan." He laughed.

Amy grew serious. "Have you ever thought of moving back to Texas?"

"Actually, yes."

"Really? So, what's stopping you?" As Ted pondered his reply, Amy studied the rugged profile of his face. It was strong and solid. The profile of a determined man.

"You know, I'm not sure."

She grew curious. "Are you reluctant to leave a job you love?"

Ted glanced over at her and chuckled. "Truth is, I don't love it. Lately, I've been wondering if the Lord even wants me here." A serious look crossed his face. "Don't laugh when I say this, but when I was a teenager, I wanted to be a pastor."

Hadn't Amy thought the very same thing? That Ted would make a great pastor? Mr. Conklin was right. She was a great discerner of character. "Why would I laugh at something as wonderful as that?"

His expression relaxed.

"Do you still want to be a pastor?"

"I've been thinking about it more recently, especially with all the chaos that's going on here."

"Why did you want to be a pastor in the first place?"

"I felt God was calling me to be."

"Well, if what you felt was a call from God, then you know what the Bible says about calls, don't you?"

Ted nodded. Her words were a confirmation. "Yeah. God doesn't change His mind about His calling."

"Right. Romans 11: 29: 'For the gifts and calling of God are without repentance.' Meaning, irrevocable.

His head jerked in her direction. "Wow! I'm impressed! How do you know so much about the Bible?"

"From Sunday School. My mother took me to church every Sunday." She didn't add that her father never went to church and that she'd stopped going, too. Amy's mind flashed back to those weekly treks to the little church in Midland, Texas. They'd saved her life after Daddy left. How easily she'd slipped away over the years! Missing one Sunday service made it easier to skip another. Before long, she'd stopped attending church altogether. Nostalgia for those comforting church services nudged her.

"My mother took my brother and me to church, too, every week. It was hard for her because my dad wasn't the church-going type." Ted changed the subject. "Well, here we are at *Piazza del Duomo*. Now, to find a parking space."

Ted drove to *Duomo Parking*, but it was filled. He finally found a spot at *Parking La Rinascente*, about a three-minute walk from the *Galleria* and the *Duomo*.

Ted helped Amy out of the car. "The plaza is usually packed on Saturdays."

"I can imagine. Besides, it's summer time, a big tourist season."

"Right."

Amy accompanied Ted into *Piazza del Duomo*. It was bustling with life. Couples, young and old, strolled arm-in-arm across the square. Grandparents sat at outdoor cafés with grandchildren playing at their feet. Starry-eyed young lovers gazed into each other's eyes while a strolling violinist played Italian love songs.

Amy's heart stirred. The very air in Italy was filled with love. It was everywhere. One could not escape it no matter where one turned. "This is amazing!"

Ted smiled. "I knew you'd like it. But this is only the beginning. The setting of the stage. The *Duomo* is the *pièce de résistance* and the spires are the dessert."

Amy laughed. "Well put, Mr. McMasters."

"Why, thank you, Miss Torelli." His broad smile melted her heart, sending a shiver coursing through her veins. What was that she detected in his eyes?

A sudden urge to take Ted's hand overtook her. She switched her shoulder bag to the shoulder between them and swallowed hard.

This was no time to let down her guard.

No time at all.

* * * *

After lunch, with Ted at her side, Amy reached the massive front doors of the *Duomo*. The large center door was already open, so they walked right in.

Ted handed the doorman two tickets he'd purchased earlier.

Upon entering the majestic structure, an overwhelming sense of awe came over Amy. She was transported to another realm, a realm of beauty beyond the natural. The cool silence of the sanctuary reverberated in her soul, bringing with it a deep sense of reverence.

Slowly, she walked toward the front of the church, admiring every detail along the way. The magnificent, marble-tiled floor. The lofty, Gothic columns. The lovely, stained-glass windows. She was ever conscious of Ted by her side, sharing the moment without words.

As she approached the altar, the stunning rose window above

it caught her eye. Its delicate design reminded her of the doilies her Italian nonna used to crochet. Perhaps Nonna had been inspired by one such rose window in a church in her native Italy.

Suddenly, Amy felt the full force of the deep roots of her Italian heritage. This was her ancestral land. The land where the roots of her life had been sown. Her Nonna's generation had transplanted those roots to America to follow their dream of freedom. And Amy had reaped the fruit of their courageous act.

Ted drew up to her side. "See that little red bulb above the apse?"

Amy looked up. "Yes."

"It marks the spot where one of the nails allegedly used in Christ's crucifixion was placed."

Amy looked in awe.

"So, what do you think?"

She turned toward him. "It literally takes my breath away."

The upward lift of the marble columns drew her attention to her Creator. The Creator from Whom she'd drifted over the years. A sudden longing to reconnect with Him engulfed her.

Strange how hurt could either draw one toward God or away from Him. In her case, hurt had driven her from the only One Who would never hurt her. The Only One Who could heal her hurt. Yet, she'd treated Him as the enemy. As the One Who'd caused her hurt. She'd pushed Him out of her life instead of allowing Him to take away her pain. She'd identified Him with her earthly father and attributed to Him the same traits as her earthly father. Because her earthly father had abandoned her, she'd believed that her heavenly Father would also abandon her. Because her earthly father had betrayed her, she'd believed that her heavenly Father would also betray her. Because her earthly father had broken her trust, she'd believed that her heavenly Father could never be trusted.

Hot tears suddenly stung her eyes.

"Are you all right?" Ted's voice startled her.

"Yes. I'm fine. This cathedral is doing a number on my emotions." She didn't dare tell him what emotions and why.

"The *Duomo* has a way of doing that." He drew closer. "I've been here many times, and the effect is the same."

"So, you come here a lot?"

"Yes. I come here when I need to get away and think. When I need to be alone." He chuckled. "Which, by the way, is pretty often. This church is a haven for me. A place where I can come and connect with who I really am."

Who are you, Ted? Suddenly she had to know.

Ted's words moved her deeply. The man before her was a man of great depth. And she had a powerful desire to explore that depth.

"Are you ready to go up to the spires?"

She nodded. "Yes. That sounds really cool."

"So, how do you want to get up there? By elevator or by taking the steps? There are two-hundred fifty steps to the rooftop, and nine-hundred-and-nineteen steps to the spires?"

She raised an eyebrow. "Nine-hundred-and-nineteen? You didn't tell me that!"

"Yes. But it's worth every step. And we can stop along the way to enjoy the scenic views of the city."

"Let's take the steps then."

Amy followed Ted to the steps that led to the *Duomo* spires. They stopped at different scenic spots on the way up. The view at each stop was extraordinary.

At one particular spot on the rooftop, Ted led Amy to a railing that overlooked the entire city of Milan. The sun had already begun its descent toward the horizon, painting the sky in brilliant hues of purple and orange.

The view took Amy's breath away. "Wow! This is magnificent!"

Ted stood by her side, only inches away. He leaned on the railing, next to her. "This elevation over the city reminds me of the temptation of Jesus, when Satan took Him to the pinnacle of the Temple and offered Him the whole world if Jesus would just bow down and worship him."

Amy turned toward Ted. "What made you think of that just now?"

Ted turned his gaze toward her. There was sorrow in his eyes. "I guess I've been questioning myself a lot lately."

"About what?"

"About what I'm doing here in Italy."

Amy studied his profile. His strong, square jaw. His long, straight nose. His sensual lips. She suddenly wanted to kiss them. Horrified at the thought, she slid farther away from him along the railing.

He turned toward her, a tender look in his eyes. "I'm seriously thinking of going back to Texas to become a pastor."

She smiled. "Great! Then become a pastor."

"You make it sound so easy."

"It is. All you need to do is decide to become one. The how will flow from that decision."

His gaze steadied on hers. "Amy, there's something I promised myself never to do again, but I'm afraid I've done it."

She tensed. "Shoot!"

He laughed at her Texan attempt to break the tension. "I promised myself I'd never fall in love again."

Amy's heart pounded. She longed for him to continue and at the same time dreaded it.

He turned fully toward her and placed his hand on hers.

Fire raced through every fiber of her being.

"I've fallen in love with you, Amy."

No. It couldn't be. It's not what she'd wanted. It's not what she'd planned. A lump rose to her throat. "I . . . uh . . . don't know what to say." What could she say? That she'd fallen in love with him, too? That's what he wanted to hear. But why could she not say it?

She couldn't say it because admitting she was in love with him would set her on a course of lifelong pain. A pain she'd tried to avoid at all costs. And so far, she'd succeeded in avoiding it.

He took both of her hands. "Do you have any feelings for me?" There was pleading in his voice. "Any at all?"

She averted his gaze. "I don't know, Ted. I'm confused. I like you as a person, but—"

"But what?"

She looked him in the eye. "I guess I'm afraid. Afraid of having a relationship with a man. I've been so hurt by men that I don't trust any of them. When I think of a relationship with a man, all I think of is that he'll betray me just as my father betrayed me."

Ted released her hands. "What would I have to do to prove to you that I'm not like your father?"

"I honestly don't know. If I trust my heart to you, I can't be sure you won't break it."

"I'd never intentionally do anything to break your heart, Amy."

Growing pensive, she turned away from him to look at the city beneath her. "When I was five years old, my father walked out on Mama and me. I was devastated. I remember one day, when I was in Kindergarten, we had a Daddy-Daughter Day. All the other fathers were already in the room, except my father. I waited and waited for him to come. I kept running to the classroom door to peek out to see if he was walking down the hall." She swallowed the sob in her throat. "But he never came." She turned toward Ted, tears rolling down her face. "He never came that day. Nor did he ever come back again. To this day, I don't know where he is. I don't know if he's dead or alive."

"I'm so sorry, Amy. That's a hurt one never forgets."

She wiped her tears away with her hand. "Enough about me. Tell me about you."

"Well, I had issues with my father, too. Ever since I was a kid, I could never do enough to please him. He'd always find fault with how I did things. Like how I mowed the lawn, or how I cleaned the garage. When I was in high school, I missed the shot that would have given my team the state championship. My dad humiliated me in public for that mistake. The memory of it still affects the way I see myself." Ted paused. "In fact, I think it had a lot to do with my breakup with a girl while I was in Afghanistan."

Amy turned toward him. "I'm sorry."

Ted told her about being jilted by Shawna shortly after he'd proposed to her, and how that had made him gun-shy of a romantic relationship.

"I hear you."

"No matter. It's all behind me now." He looked at her. "As is your situation with your father."

"But is it really? Sometimes these kinds of things take a long time to heal." She lowered her eyes. "And sometimes they never heal at all."

By the time they'd shared their hearts, the radiant purple-orange sun had approached the horizon. Dusk settled over the *Duomo* rooftop.

Ted looked at her. "I think we'd better head out to dinner. I don't want to be stuck up here for the night when they lock up the *Duomo*."

Amy smiled. If she ever got stuck anywhere, she'd want it to be with Ted.

He took her hands and drew her to himself.

Amy's heart raced.

In an instant, his warm lips were on hers, driving out all fear. Suddenly her world shifted. Suddenly things between her and Ted were no longer the same. Suddenly she knew she loved him.

He released her and smiled. "Now let's go eat. I hope you're hungry. *La Porta Rossa* has a fantastic menu."

But Amy had no appetite. A warm glow had settled into the pit of her stomach. It filled her completely, leaving no room for food.

As they made their way down the steps to the plaza, all she could think about was what had she gotten herself into.

Perhaps it was time to give Sara another call.

Chapter Ten

Taking her by the elbow, Ted led Amy through the main door of *La Porta Rossa* Restaurant. His heart thrilled at the prospect of sharing a special meal with her.

True to its name, *La Porta Rossa* had a rustic, red front door that opened into a delightfully charming space with only a few tables and a very romantic *ambiance*. Red-checkered tablecloths covered the tables. On each table sat a small, flickering votive candle that added a touch of warmth to the atmosphere. Along the red walls hung pictures of numerous celebrities who had frequented the restaurant and left their accolades.

The place was bustling with the rapid movement of waiters balancing large trays *en route* to their tables, the loud chatter of diners engaged in lively conversation, and the soft whispers of lovers whose eyes saw only each other. A tuxedoed violinist made his way from table to table, smiling warmly as he serenaded the international *clientèle* with Italy's most famous love songs.

Ted stopped before the *maître d'* station and drew Amy toward him. His soul still quivered at the tenderness of her kiss and the way she had yielded. Had he been wrong in kissing her? What if word got back to the office? Would his action be considered inappropriate? Worthy of dismissal?

He squelched the thought. Now was no time to worry. Now was the time to enjoy a special dinner with the woman he loved. He'd deal with any consequences later, if there were any.

"*Buona sera.* Good evening." The *maître d'* greeted them with a warm smile.

Ted returned the greeting. "*Buona sera.* Do you have a small table for two available in a far corner?"

"Yes. This way, please." The *maître d'* led them to a cozy table for two at the far end of the large room. It sat in a small alcove, away from the other tables. "Will this be all right?"

"Perfect." Ted was pleased to have a space where he and Amy could talk privately.

He helped Amy with her chair while the *maître d'* placed two menus on the table. "Your waiter will be with you momentarily." He then smiled and left.

Ted took his seat opposite Amy. The light of the candle, reflected in her eyes, enhanced the beauty of her face. His heart stirred. "So, what did you think of the *Duomo*?"

"There are no words to describe it."

She seemed troubled.

"Amy, I'm sorry I kissed you."

Tears filled her eyes.

"No. That's a lie. I'm not sorry I kissed you, but I'm sorry I kissed you when I did, if you know what I mean."

"I'm not sorry, Ted." Her words were barely a whisper.

He took her hand, "Then, what's the problem? You look upset."

"The problem is I'm scared. I'm scared of what's happening between us. I can't let it happen. I promised myself I'd never let it happen. And now it's happening."

"I know what you mean. I made myself a similar promise."

She gave him a surprised look. "You did?"

Before Ted could reply, the waiter came to their table. When he noticed Amy's tears, he pulled out a clean white handkerchief from his shirt pocket and handed it to her. "Compliments of *La Porta Rossa.*"

Amy laughed. "*Grazie*. I needed that."

"*Prego*. You're welcome. Are you ready for me to take your order?"

Ted looked up apologetically. "I'm sorry. We haven't even looked at our menus yet."

The waiter smiled a knowing smile. "Why look at a menu when you have this lovely woman to look at?"

Amy laughed at the compliment.

Ted opened his menu. "You're right. Would you mind coming back in a few moments?"

"Not at all. Anything in the name of *amore*."

The waiter left momentarily.

Amy chuckled and opened her menu. "Italians are certainly the most love-minded people I've ever met."

"And there's nothing wrong with that. Maybe we could learn something from them."

They chose two entrées.

Ted caught the waiter's attention, and he returned to take their order.

The waiter smiled. "So, what would the *signorina* like this evening?"

"I'll take the *Salmone alla Griglia* with roasted potatoes and asparagus spears."

He turned toward Ted. "And you, sir?"

"I'll have the *Veal Scallopine* with *Risotto alla Milanese*."

"Very good. Thank you." The waiter retrieved the menus and left.

Ted resumed their conversation. "Anyway, I made a similar promise six years ago when I was jilted by my former girlfriend."

Compassion filled Amy's eyes. "I'm sorry."

"Thanks. I promised myself I'd never fall in love again. It wasn't worth the pain."

"I hear you."

He leaned forward and caressed her hand. "So here I go again, falling in love with you."

Her eyes glistened with tears, but she remained silent.

"I kissed you because I love you, Amy. For no other reason. You've got to believe that."

Her tears now rolled down her cheeks. "I do, Ted. I can tell you love me. I see it in your eyes."

"Then what are you afraid of?"

"I'm afraid that one day, you'll stop loving me. That you'll betray me just like my father."

"I will never betray you, Amy."

"That's what my father said. That he'd never do anything to hurt Mama and me." A sob escaped her. "But he did."

Ted squeezed her hand. "I'm sorry your father abandoned you. I truly am."

"And I'm sorry you were jilted."

Ted smiled. "I'm not. Otherwise, I wouldn't have met you."

Amy blushed.

Just then the waiter returned with their orders.

Amy looked at her platter. "This looks delicious."

"It is. Their salmon is the best I've had since I've been in Italy."

"Your veal looks good, too."

Amy took a bite of the tender salmon. Grilled in butter and seasoned with a medley of herbs, it melted in her mouth. "Heavenly!" She swallowed the morsel and smiled. "How's yours?"

"Delicious as well."

She changed the subject. "I called Interpol."

"Oh? And what did they say?" Ted studied her. It was obvious she wasn't ready to go on with any discussion of where their relationship was headed from here. He would save that discussion for another more appropriate time.

"They want to meet with me Monday morning."

"Do you want me to come with you? I'm scheduled to go to Torino Monday afternoon, but I'm available in the morning."

She hesitated. "I do, but Interpol won't allow it because you're one of the three who have access to the ledger."

Ted's stomach tensed. "I get it. I can't say I like it, but I understand their reasoning."

"I can't share much more than that, except that I called Mr. Conklin, and he gave me the go-ahead to meet with them."

"I'll be praying for you."

Amy chuckled.

"What's so funny?"

"It strikes me funny that you'll be praying for me in a case that involves you as a potential guilty party."

"Well, my conscience is clear because I'm innocent."

She gave him a long, studied look.

An uneasy feeling overwhelmed Ted. "You still have doubts about my innocence, don't you?"

She was slow to answer. "I don't know what to think anymore, Ted. More than anything else, I want you to be innocent. But I just don't know who's guilty and who's not."

His heart broke. She didn't trust him. And how could they build a relationship without trust? "I see."

Her eyes pleaded with him. "I can't lie to you, Ted."

"I know you can't." He swallowed hard. "It's okay. When I put myself in your shoes, I totally understand where you're coming from. You've known me for only two weeks. How can I expect you to trust me?"

"I'm sorry, Ted. I truly am."

Ted swallowed the lump in his throat. There was that old feeling again. The feeling of rejection. The feeling he was a loser. The day that had begun with such promise was fast turning sour.

The waiter returned. "Are you ready for dessert?"

Ted looked at Amy.

She shook her head.

"Thanks, but we're going to skip dessert."

The waiter looked surprised. "Very well, then. Here is your

check." He retrieved Ted's check from his notepad and handed it to him. "I'll take your credit card when you're ready."

After Ted paid the bill and left a tip, he led Amy out of the restaurant, all the while hoping he wasn't leading her out of his heart as well.

* * * *

On Monday morning, Amy made her way to the offices of the International Criminal Police Organization, commonly known as Interpol, in downtown Milan. Her stomach jittered at the prospect of having to meet with them alone. Armed with all of her data thus far, she'd carefully prepared her presentation and hoped that Interpol would be able to start an investigation. A lengthy phone conversation with Mr. Conklin over the weekend had briefed her as to how to handle herself as a representative of Enson Pharmaceuticals.

She entered the tall, high-rise building where Interpol's offices were located. She took the elevator to the second floor and made her way down the long corridor to the last office on the right. Upon entering, a gracious receptionist greeted her.

"Good morning. I'm Amy Torelli. I have an appointment with Mr. Salvatore Addevico."

The receptionist smiled. "Yes. Mr. Addevico is expecting you."

In a few moments, the receptionist ushered Amy into Mr. Addevico's office.

"Miss Torelli." Mr. Addevico rose, shook her hand, and greeted her with a warm smile. "Welcome to Interpol."

"Thank you." Amy instantly felt at ease.

"Please have a seat." He motioned toward a chair in a corner of the office and took the one opposite hers.

Amy placed her purse on the floor and settled into her chair.

Mr. Addevico spoke first. "So, I understand you are here on what looks like a case of embezzlement at Enson Pharmaceuticals."

"Yes." She related to him her discoveries during her audit of the past two weeks and then handed him her findings.

Mr. Addevico nodded. "When you mentioned Roberto Manero over the phone, I wasn't surprised. We've been having major problems with him here in Italy regarding drug trafficking. What better place to get large supplies of drugs than from a pharmaceutical company that makes narcotics, no?"

"I see your point."

"Just so you're prepared, we will require access to the Enson computer."

"I can give you my login information, but I do not have the usernames and passwords for anyone else."

"No problem. We will retrieve the other usernames and passwords from the computer itself."

"Really?"

Mr. Addevico smiled. "Yes, we have our ways."

Amy smiled in return. "I guess you do."

"Tell me. Who are the suspects at Enson who could be involved in this crime?" He poised his pen to write on the legal pad he held on his lap.

"Giorgio Bassetti, the president, Silvia Villano, his personal assistant, and—" Her heart clenched. If she mentioned Ted, his reputation could be ruined for good.

Mr. Addevico looked up. "And?"

"Ted McMasters, the vice-president." The life flowed out of Amy's heart.

"Do you think all three are guilty?"

"No. All three have made entries in the ledger, but I don't think Mr. McMasters is guilty."

"What makes you say that?"

She couldn't say because she was in love with him. "He just seems to be a man of integrity. Although," she hastened to add, "one can never tell."

Mr. Addevico eyed her intently. "You're right. I've been in this business long enough to know that things are not always what they seem." He gave a cursory look at the data she'd brought. "I will peruse these carefully this afternoon and then get back to you." He rose. "Be assured that we will get on the matter right away."

Amy rose, too. "Thank you, Mr. Addevico. I appreciate your time and expertise."

"When do you return to New York?"

"Next week."

"I may need to contact you while you're here and once you're back in the States. Do you have a cell phone number I may use to reach you?"

She withdrew one of her business cards from her shoulder bag and handed it to him. "All of my contact information is on the card."

"Thank you." He extended his hand. "It was a pleasure to meet you. Know that you are doing a great work in helping us to stamp out crime."

The compliment touched her. "Thank you. And so are you."

* * * *

The day after Amy's meeting with Interpol, Silvia looked up inquiringly from her computer at the gentleman who walked into the president's office.

He showed her his ID. "I'm Salvatore Addevico from Interpol."

Silvia's blood turned to ice.

Mr. Addevico smiled. "And you are?"

"I'm Silvia Villano, Mr. Bassetti's personal assistant."

"It's a pleasure to meet you, Miss Villano."

Silvia's stomach clenched. "Is Mr. Bassetti expecting you?" She glanced at Giorgio's calendar. "I don't see your name on his schedule."

"No. But I would like to speak with him."

"He's not here right now." Giorgio would be back soon. She had to figure out a way to warn him.

"Do you know when he will return?"

"He should be back shortly, but I don't know for sure. Would you like to schedule an appointment with him?"

"No. I'd like to ask you a few questions, if you don't mind."

She couldn't say she did mind. That would make her look as though she had something to hide. "What is this all about?"

Mr. Addevico slipped his ID card back into his wallet. "It's about a possible case of embezzlement here at your company."

Silvia feigned surprise. "Embezzlement?" She felt Mr. Addevico's penetrating gaze.

"Yes, embezzlement."

She shifted in her chair. "What questions do you have?"

He pointed to a nearby chair. "May I sit down? This might take a few moments."

She hesitated. "Yes." A chill ran through her. This could be the beginning of the end. She had to protect herself at all costs.

"We've received a report from an auditor sent here from your New York headquarters to audit the books."

Silvia's muscles tensed. So, Amy had reported her findings to Interpol. Did Giorgio know? "Yes, Miss Torelli has been auditing our books for the past two weeks."

"Then you may know she has discovered several suspicious entries in the ledgers."

"No. I didn't know." The lie burned on her lips.

"Well, now you do." He smiled at her, all the while giving her a piercing gaze, as though looking straight into her soul.

Silvia tensed. "So, what does this mean?"

"It means we need to find out why the discrepancies and who is responsible for them."

Her stomach roiled. "Well, I think Mr. Bassetti is the person who may be able to answer those questions for you."

"I think you may be able to answer them as well."

She began to protest but thought the better of it.

Mr. Addevico continued to probe. "Are you not one of the three people who has access to the ledgers in order to post entries?"

"Yes." Bile climbed up her throat. Amy must have revealed that information to him.

"And when you make entries, you use a personal username and password known only to you, correct?"

"Yes."

"We will need your personal username and password to verify which entries were made by you."

"But why do you need to verify them?"

"It's to protect you, Miss Villano. You do realize, don't you, that you are one of three possible suspects in this case?"

Her stomach churned. "No. I did not realize that." A second lie.

"Well, I'm sorry to say, you are. But, if you fully cooperate with us, you have nothing to be concerned about. Our job is not only to discover the guilty but also to protect the innocent."

The smile he gave her only incited her panic. "I think I should wait until Mr. Bassetti returns before I give you any more information. I don't have the authority to make those kinds of decisions."

"I understand. Since you said he would be back shortly, I'll wait."

What should she do? "Would you like a cup of coffee while you wait?"

"That would be very nice."

She poured him a cup of coffee from the office coffeepot and handed it to him. "Cream and sugar are on the credenza behind you."

"Thank you."

"Would you excuse me please while I use the restroom?" What could he say? No?

While Mr. Addevico stirred his coffee, she slipped her cell phone into her pocket and went to the restroom. Once in there, she tapped on Giorgio's number.

He answered right away.

"Giorgio, there's a man from Interpol in the office waiting to see you." Her voice was a whisper.

"Don't give him any information. I'll be there right away."

She ended the call and returned to her desk. While Mr. Addevico pored through a magazine, she typed an email to Roberto Manero. "Interpol here. Brace yourself for trouble. ~ Silvia." Just as she hit SEND, Giorgio walked into the office.

Mr. Addevico rose. "I take it you are Mr. Bassetti?"

Giorgio eyed him suspiciously. "Yes. And you are?"

Mr. Addevico showed his ID. "Salvatore Addevico from Interpol."

"Come into my office, please." He turned to Silvia. "You, too, Silvia. I'll need you to take notes."

Taking his coffee cup with him, Mr. Addevico followed Giorgio into his office.

Giorgio pointed to the chair in front of his desk. "Please. Have a seat."

"Thank you."

Giorgio sat down and folded his hands over his stomach. His face looked ashen and taut.

Pen and notebook in hand, Silvia pulled up a chair to his left.

Giorgio leaned forward. "So, what brings you to Enson Italia?"

"A possible case of embezzlement. Your auditor, Amy Torelli, has discovered some suspicious transactions in your books that point to embezzlement of possible international proportions. Hence, her contacting Interpol."

Giorgio raised an eyebrow. "I see." He chewed on his lip. "I knew nothing of this before now and am, frankly, quite surprised that Miss Torelli did not inform me of it."

"Her job is to report, not to accuse. Interpol's job is to investigate and to discover the culprits of a crime."

Giorgio's face turned pale. For a long moment, he did not speak. "Do you have any suspects yet?"

"We have three."

"May I ask who they are?"

"You, Miss Villano, and Mr. Ted McMasters. The three people in your office authorized to make entries in the ledgers."

"But what if someone else got into the ledgers?"

"Each of you has a unique private username and password, correct?"

"Yes. That is correct."

"None of you has shared that username with the others, correct?"

"Not that I'm aware of."

"Then any one of you could be guilty of embezzlement."

"But how can you prove who is the guilty one?" Giorgio obviously caught himself. "If, indeed, any one of the three of us is guilty?"

"That is something left to us. But let me assure you that the guilty one will be discovered."

Giorgio glanced at Silvia. "Be assured, Mr. Addevico, that this office will fully cooperate with your investigation. What do you need from me?"

"I need to access the computer in question and the ledgers involved."

Giorgio turned to Silvia. "Silvia, please take Mr. Addevico to the computer room and show him how to access the computer and the ledgers."

"Yes, sir."

Silvia led Mr. Addevico to the small computer room, turned on the computer, and logged in for him. "If you have any questions, let me know."

"Thank you."

"When you've finished, simply log off, lock the door behind you, and return the key to me in the main office."

"Will do."

Mr. Addevico settled into the chair and began his investigation.

As Silvia turned to leave, she smiled in relief that she'd recently changed her entries to make them look as though Ted had entered them.

my hadn't spoken with Ted since Saturday night, and it was now Wednesday morning. He'd been gone from the office for two days to attend to some company business in Torino. But today he would be back. Although she'd hoped to hear from him, he was probably still troubled over their conversation at *La Porta Rossa*. But what else could she have done? The continual fear of being viewed as biased in the audit worried her. If Silvia and Giorgio discovered that there were feelings between her and Ted, the whole audit would come under suspicion and Amy's job would be on the line.

She sat in the computer room, trying to keep her mind on preparing additional reports for Interpol. One by one, she reviewed the suspicious entries, making note on her legal pad of the dates and times of each entry. But as she worked, her mind kept wandering. Over and over again, she pictured Ted's distress at the way she'd rejected him at the restaurant the previous Saturday night. The forlorn look on his face seared her soul. In essence, she'd told him she didn't trust him. As a result, she'd hurt him badly. And ever since, she'd kicked herself for the way she'd treated him.

Why couldn't she let her heart trust him? In the two weeks she'd known him, he'd kept his word to her in every situation. What horrible thing kept holding her back? Kept preventing her from yielding to his love? Yes, Daddy had abandoned her. Yes, he'd broken her trust. But what did her father have to do with Ted? She couldn't just dump all men into the same category, could she?

Yet, that was precisely what she was doing. She was blaming Ted for her father's betrayal. She was projecting onto Ted the mistrust she had for her father. How would she like it if Ted did that to her? She wouldn't like it at all.

She blinked her eyes several times to clear away the blurriness. Looking at numbers on a computer all day wasn't the best thing for one's vision. She gently rubbed her eyes and then returned to her work. She'd stop by Ted's office over lunch break to see how he was doing. To apologize. To tell him she'd chosen to trust him.

She'd make things right between them, all the while keeping her professional distance. Her only prayer was that it wasn't too late.

* * * *

Amy found Ted sitting behind a tall pile of papers on his desk. "Hey!" Her heart pounded. Would he welcome her or reject her?

He smiled. "Hey, yourself!"

A wave of relief flooded her soul. He wasn't angry with her. He acted as though the Saturday night fiasco hadn't even happened at all. "How was your trip?"

"Uneventful. Same old, same old. The Torino office needed some help with a hiring situation. But we got the problem under control."

"As you always do." She smiled at him.

His eyes widened. "Why, thank you for the compliment."

"Do you have a minute?"

He nodded. "How about we grab a cup of coffee in the cafeteria?"

"Sure. But it won't be your mother's brew."

He laughed.

So, things were still the same between them. Isn't that how it was with love? Nothing could destroy it if it were genuine.

Amy poured two cups of espresso and brought them to a small

table at the far end of the cafeteria where she and Ted sat down. She took two teaspoons of sugar from the sugar bowl at the center of the table.

Ted followed suit. "How was the rest of your weekend?"

So, Saturday night was still on his mind after all. "Miserable."

He looked up. "Mine, too."

The sad look on his face broke her heart. "Ted, I'm so sorry. I've been doing a lot of thinking the last few days. I haven't been fair to you. I've been blaming you for my father's betrayal. I haven't given you a chance to prove your trustworthiness. I didn't realize it before, but I've lumped all men into the same category. Will you forgive me? *Can* you forgive me?"

His eyes glistened. "Of course, I forgive you." He took her hand in his.

She glanced around the cafeteria to make sure they weren't being seen or overheard, but the place was empty this time of day.

"Amy, I love you. Nothing can ever change that. And you'd make me the happiest man in the world if you loved me, too. But I can't force you to love me. I can't force you to trust me. It has to come naturally."

A lump rose to her throat. "I do love you, Ted." She squeezed his hand and smiled. "You have the unique distinction of being the first man I've ever loved since my father betrayed me."

He looked at her intently. "Have you forgiven your father?"

Ted's question caught her up short. "I don't really know."

"Maybe that's been part of your problem in trusting me. You haven't yet forgiven your father."

She pondered his words. "Maybe. But remember that I've known you only two weeks. That's not enough time to build trust in a relationship."

"Well, if it isn't the two lovebirds of Enson Italia." Silvia's strident voice suddenly broke the solemnity of the moment.

Amy quickly withdrew her hand from Ted's. Neither one of them had seen Silvia enter the cafeteria. Amy tensed.

Ted jumped in. "Excuse me, Silvia, but Miss Torelli and I were discussing a private matter."

Silvia gave him a smirk. "Yes. That's quite obvious, especially given that you were holding hands."

Ted stood. "And what's that to you?"

"You know company policy. No romantic relationships among employees."

"Yes. And it might do you good to obey that policy yourself."

Silvia's face turned pale. "I don't know what you're talking about."

"I think you do. Are you so naïve as to think that all of Enson Italia doesn't know about you and Giorgio?"

Silvia grew defensive. "There's nothing between Giorgio and me."

"You're right. Nothing except ten years of your serving as his mistress."

She narrowed her eyes. "How dare you?"

Ted glared at her. "I think you'd do well to keep your nose out of people's personal business."

His words hit their mark as Silvia turned on her heels and left.

Ted sat back down.

Amy gave him a nervous look. "Do you think she'll report us?"

"So, what if she does? I don't really care. I'm about to leave this place anyway."

"You are?"

"Yes."

"When did you decide that?"

"When I kissed you on the rooftop of the *Duomo*."

Amy's heart stirred at the memory.

Ted took her hand again and gazed deeply into her eyes. "Amy Torelli, will you marry me?"

Amy's heart exploded with joy. Tears rushed to her eyes. "Yes, Ted, I'll marry you. I love you, and I've chosen to trust you."

* * * *

Amy's impromptu visit to his office had made Ted's day. Although he'd planned to ask her to marry him, he hadn't planned to do so in the cafeteria. Yet, given their conversation, it seemed like the right time, and he had no regrets. In a single moment, he'd gone from being in the depths of despair to being in the heights of joy.

I told you I would direct your steps.

Ted smiled. God had once again shown His faithfulness to His Word.

Ted's decision to leave Enson and fulfill God's calling on his life to become a pastor had been slow but sure in coming. His questions regarding the ledger entries, culminating in the suspicion of embezzlement, had sealed his decision that the corporate world wasn't for him.

Meeting Amy had helped to crystallize things in Ted's mind. Things like motives and priorities. Learning of her struggles with seeking approval, Ted had discovered the insight and the courage to face his own struggles. When all was said and done, the only thing that mattered in life was relationship. First, relationship with God and then, relationship with others. And, if God willed, with one special other.

He sat in front of his computer, formulating a letter of resignation to Giorgio and to Mr. Conklin. Gone was his dream of one day becoming company president. Had it really ever been his dream? Or had it been a way of gaining his father's approval?

Maybe he and Amy were more alike than he'd realized. Maybe, in deciding to marry each other, they had both ditched the need for human approval because they'd discovered they both had the approval of the only One Who really mattered—God the Father Himself. Having His approval made the approval of others a gift, not a necessity. That realization had been a long time in coming, but it had come. Amy had been delighted when he'd told her he was going to hand in his letter of resignation, return to Texas, and become a pastor.

Ted re-read what he'd written so far. He'd give Enson the required month's notice and then pack up his bags for Texas. His mother had mentioned in passing that the pastor of her little church in the town where he'd grown up had decided to retire, and the church would soon need another pastor. He'd start there and see where the Lord would lead.

Truth be told, he'd have no problem leaving the corporate world. Yes, he'd learned a lot, but his heart was in another place. And now that Amy had agreed to marry him, her heart would be in the same place. Together, they'd do great things for the Kingdom of God.

His heart at peace, he finished the letter and printed three copies—one for Giorgio, one for Mr. Conklin, and one for himself. Then, affixing his signature to them, he placed them in envelopes and dropped two of them into the outgoing mail file.

Relieved that his resignation letter was finished, Ted rose for a coffee break when his cell phone rang. He looked at the caller ID: Interpol.

His muscles tensed. Why would Interpol be calling him?

He shrugged off the concern and answered the phone. "*Pronto.* Hello. This is Ted McMasters."

The voice on the other end was business-like. "Mr. McMasters, this is Salvatore Addevico of Interpol."

"Yes, Mr. Addevico."

"Would it be possible for you to stop by my office for a few moments this afternoon? There's something very important I need to discuss with you."

Ted hesitated. "Uh . . . yes. I could stop by right after lunch, at about one o'clock. Would that work for you?"

"One o'clock is perfect. I'll see you then."

Ted ended the call and slipped his cell phone into his pocket. He'd hesitated to ask Mr. Addevico the reason he wanted to see him. Frankly, Ted had been too nervous to ask. But why should he be nervous? He had nothing to hide.

Yet, fear niggled at the edge of his brain. Maybe he was nervous because Silvia had something to hide. And, knowing Silvia, whatever she had to hide could end up being a big problem for him.

Maybe he should talk with Amy before he left for the Interpol office.

He logged off his computer and turned it off. Then, informing his secretary he'd be out for most of the afternoon, he made his way to the computer room. When he arrived, Amy was sitting, as usual, in front of the large screen.

Ted shut the door behind him. "Amy, how busy are you? I need to talk with you."

She turned and faced him. "Sure. I can break away for a few minutes. What's up?"

He sat down in the chair next to hers. He resisted the urge to take her in his arms and smother her with kisses. "I got a call from Interpol. They want to meet with me this afternoon."

Amy's eyebrows furrowed. "Did they say why?"

"No. Only that they had something very important to discuss with me. I have no clue what it is, but I have a feeling it's not good."

"You have nothing to worry about, Ted. You said you're innocent. You can go with a clean conscience."

"Yes. I can. But it's Silvia I don't trust."

"What do you mean?"

"I think she's up to something."

"Like what?"

"Like protecting her skin and scoring mine."

Amy's face paled. "Do you think she's that vicious?"

"I wouldn't put anything past her."

"But what could she possibly do to harm you?"

Ted drew in a deep breath. "She could blackmail me, that's what she could do."

"But how?"

"I don't know how. I just have this uneasy feeling she's up to no good." Ted took her hands. "Would you pray for me?"

It had been a long time since Amy had prayed. Her mind went back to the days when she'd hear Mama praying in the wee hours of the morning, crying out to God for help. She tried to remember Mama's words, but only bits and pieces came back to her. "Sure, I'll pray for you."

She held Ted's hands. "Lord Jesus, we need Your help." She hesitated, not knowing what to say next. "Help us, Lord. Amen." That's all she could say, but somehow, she knew it was enough. After all, wasn't God more concerned about one's heart than about the words one used to pray to Him?

"Thanks." Ted gave her a peck on the cheek. "I'll call you as soon as I'm done." He gave her a penetrating look. "I love you, Amy."

"I love you, too, Ted."

Her words landed like water on arid ground, reviving him for the task ahead.

Chapter Twelve

"I saw them holding hands with my own eyes!" Silvia strutted in front of Giorgio's desk. "With my very own eyes, I tell you!" She pointed emphatically at her two eyes.

"So, what do you want me to do about it?" Giorgio sat calmly in his swivel chair, hands folded on his lap.

"I want you to fire them both."

"But, Silvia. Think about what you're saying. We have no case against them."

She put her hands on her hips. "But it's company policy that there be no romantic relationships among employees."

"And who's to stop it?"

She placed both hands on the edge of his desk, leaned over, and glared at him. "Giorgio Bassetti, you're the president. You stop them!"

"You know if I try to stop them, it would be like casting the first stone."

"Since when have you become so religious?"

"I'm not trying to be religious. I'm trying to be fair. How can I fire two employees holding hands when you and I have done far more than that? I may be wicked, but I'm not a hypocrite. I cannot accuse another human being of something for which I myself am guilty."

Silvia's insides flamed. The look on his face told her she'd hit a chord. A major chord.

"Silvia, I am going to let this matter drop." He paused. "Frankly, I'm happy for Ted and Amy. I think they make the perfect couple."

She exploded. "The perfect couple! Are you crazy? That

woman from New York is a seductress. She's seduced Ted into thinking he's in love with her."

"But maybe he is. And, if so, what difference does it make to you?"

"Humph!" She waved a dismissive hand at him. "I've had it with you, Giorgio. You will never understand me."

"I understand you only two well, Silvia. When you can't get your way, you make it miserable for everyone around you."

Giorgio had read her right, and she didn't like it. Not one bit.

She tried to compose herself. "Giorgio, listen to me. The matter of Ted and Amy is insignificant in light of the situation with the embezzlement," she lied. "If you and I are implicated in the crime, we could go to jail."

"Not with Manero in the mix. He promised to protect us."

"I'm not so sure about that. If we're not careful, Manero could end up in jail with us."

Giorgio sat up straight. "What do you mean?"

"I mean that Interpol is on to Manero."

Giorgio's eyes narrowed. "How did that happen?"

"There are several checks made out to him in the ledger. Do you remember we decided to use his company as a front for funneling drugs and pharmaceutical profits in the guise of paying for a service?"

Giorgio nodded. "I remember." He hesitated. "Maybe that wasn't such a good idea."

"It wasn't. In fact, it was a stupid idea. He's a big name in the Mafia. Too easily recognizable."

Giorgio sighed. "Well, it's too late now. We'll have to deal with the mess we've made."

"But what if we can't?"

"Then let the chips fall where they may."

She spat at him. "I can't believe you! You're willing to risk our going to jail because you don't have the guts to stop it?"

He rose and moved toward her, taking her into his arms. "What do you want me to do?" He stroked her hair.

She pulled away. "Don't you realize the seriousness of the situation? If Amy discovers what we' done, we're dead meat."

He dropped his hand to his side. "I think we're already dead meat."

"What do you mean?"

"I think it's too late, Silvia. I think Amy is already on to us."

Silvia shuddered. "I'm done with you, Giorgio. Done! Do you hear me?"

"Yes, I hear you." He lowered his voice. "Until you need me the next time."

But this time, Silvia promised herself there would be no next time.

* * * *

On Wednesday afternoon, Ted entered the main lobby of the Interpol Building and checked the marquis for the location of Mr. Addevico's office. Second floor. Suite 202. He opted for the steps instead of the elevator and made his way to the office at the far end of the hall.

A young receptionist greeted him.

"I'm Ted McMasters. I have an appointment with Mr. Addevico at one o'clock."

The young woman smiled. "I'll tell him you're here."

In a few moments, she returned. "Mr. Addevico is expecting you. You may go in now." She pointed to a room a short distance down the hall and on the right.

"Thank you." Ted walked the few steps to Mr. Addevico's office and entered.

Mr. Addevico rose to greet him. "Hello, Mr. McMasters. It's a pleasure to meet you."

"Likewise." Ted shook his extended hand.

"Please sit down." Mr. Addevico pointed to a cushioned, straight-backed chair in front of his desk.

Ted sat down and placed his hands on the armrest.

"I'm sure you're wondering why I've called you here."

Ted smiled. "Yes. Although I have my hunches."

"It has to do with the embezzlement case at your company."

Ted listened attentively. "It's of grave concern to me as the vice-president."

"As well it should be."

"I suppose you know that your auditor, Amy Torelli, came to us, with the approval of your international president, Mr. Wendell Conklin, to request our help in what clearly looks like a major crime that may have global implications."

Ted nodded.

"Since you are one of the three people permitted to make entries to the ledger, I need to ask you a few questions."

"Shoot!"

Mr. Addevico raised a questioning eyebrow.

"Oh, I'm sorry. That's an expression we use in Texas to mean 'Go right ahead. Ask.'"

Mr. Addevico chuckled. "You Americans sometimes stump me with your unusual turns of phrases." He looked at his papers on his desk. "In any case, I need to know from you your specific role in making the entries. Do you make most of them, some of them, only certain categories of them? And, I also need to know if, when making the entries, you had any questions about their legitimacy."

Ted gathered his thoughts. "Well, to answer your first question, my specific role has been to enter all payments for purchase orders for office supplies. That doesn't mean I haven't, on occasion, entered payments for other categories. But my primary area of entry has been for office supplies."

"I see." Mr. Addevico made some notes on his legal pad.

"As for any questions about the legitimacy of the payments, I had no occasion to question them since I read only my own entries. But when revenues began to fall, I became suspicious and used my authority as vice-president to investigate other entries. That's when I noticed unusual entries and reported them to Mr. Conklin. Frankly, I didn't want to come across as an incompetent VP who didn't know what was going on. And I didn't want headquarters to think I was sleeping on the job."

"What did you discover when you checked the entire ledger?"

"I discovered several discrepancies that raised red flags. Enough red flags to warrant my contacting Mr. Conklin to report my findings and concerns."

"Would you kindly elaborate on the nature of the discrepancies? Did they have to do with amounts, payees, categories of purchase?"

"All three, actually. But, particularly, the payees. I did not recognize many of them as vendors with whom we do business. Moreover, they were vendors with whom we would have no reason to do business."

"Can you name some of them?"

"Yes. The Lafayette Hotel in Lugano, Switzerland, is one. The Lafayette is a resort, and Enson has no occasion to entertain guests at hotel resorts. Another is an office supply company by the name of *Prodotti Uffici.* There were several entries for this company for notebooks that we do not use at Enson. All of our documents are on computer."

Mr. Addevico made note of Ted's observations.

"So, where do we go from here?" Ted asked.

"You yourself don't go anywhere. You must stay in Milan until further notice. We can't rule out anyone's implication in the embezzlement, including yours, sir. Especially since you are one of the three people most closely involved with the ledgers."

Ted's heart sank. He'd hoped that his visit with Mr. Addevico would have settled his innocence once and for all. "What is the next step in the investigation?"

"Each of the three of you—Giorgio, Silvia, and you—will be interrogated by various Interpol officials. Then, based on the interrogation, the matter will very likely go to trial, unless, of course, the culprit confesses."

"So, we're talking about weeks, months?"

"Maybe years."

The hair on the nape of Ted's neck stood up. "Years? I can't stick around in Italy for years!"

"Let's take things one step at a time. As part of my job, I must give you the worst-case scenario. But, normally, cases are resolved in no more than a matter of a few months. Maybe weeks."

Even that time frame was too long for Ted. It would mean not seeing Amy for months after her return to the States. It would mean delaying their wedding. It would mean not being able to leave Enson to take a pastorate in Texas.

It would mean everything he didn't want it to mean.

"I guess that's all I can do. Take things one step at a time."

Mr. Addevico nodded and rose. "Thank you for your time, Mr. McMasters. I will be in touch with you shortly."

Ted rose as well. "Thank you." He shook Mr. Addevico's extended hand and then turned to leave.

"Mr. McMasters?"

"Yes?" Ted looked back.

"I truly hope, for your sake, that the matter is settled quickly."

"Thank you, sir." He gave Mr. Addevico a weak smile. "So do I."

* * * *

While Ted was at the Interpol office, Amy called Sara. Because of the time difference between Milan and New York, Sara would be getting ready to leave for the office.

Amy tapped on her best friend's phone number. At the sound of Sara's bubbly voice, Amy's stress level suddenly plummeted.

"Hey! To what do I owe this surprise?"

"I just needed to hear your voice."

"Uh-oh. You say that only when you're upset."

Sara read her like a book.

"What's up, girlfriend?"

Amy sighed. "You're right. I'm upset." She stretched out her legs on the retaining wall in the park across the street from the Enson office, one of her favorite places to unwind. Amy proceeded with caution, anticipating Sara's reaction. "I'm engaged to be married."

Sara's silence screamed in Amy's ear.

"Did you hear me?"

"Yes. I heard you. I'm trying to think of what to say. If I say, 'I told you so,' you'll kill me when you get back. *If* you come back, that is. If I don't say anything, you'll ask me why I'm not saying anything."

"Okay. Okay. You did tell me so. I'll eat crow."

"So, tell me why you called me. Did Ted hurt you? If he did, why did you agree to marry him?"

Amy smiled at the barrage of questions, so typical of Sara. "No, he didn't hurt me, but I'm just waiting for the shoe to drop."

"Amy, it's not fair to Ted to expect the worst of him."

Amy changed position to dangling her legs over the retaining wall. "Whose side are you on anyway?"

"I'm on the side of truth. The best side to be on."

If there was one thing Amy loved about Sara, it was her commitment to truth. That commitment made Sara a good sounding board for wise advice. "You're right. That's the reason I called you. I need some truth."

"Do you really want truth, or are you just pretending you want truth? Some people pretend they want truth, but don't really want it."

Whoa! Sara had this annoying habit of hitting the nail on the head. And when she did, it hurt. Did Amy really want the truth? Or was she only pretending to want it?

Amy sighed. All right already with the twenty questions. "How does a gal know if she really wants the truth?"

"I guess she can tell by her answer to this question: Is she willing to accept the truth, whether she likes it or not?"

Amy drew in a deep breath. "That, I am."

"Then tell me why you've agreed to marry a guy when you've known him for only two weeks."

"Because I feel as though I've known him all of my life. We're from the same area in West Texas. We're both Christians. And we both are tired of the corporate world and want to live a simple, quiet life."

"Well, you've got the main thing right: you're both Christians. That's non-negotiable for you as a Christian. So, you can check that one off your list."

Amy laughed. "So, you're making a list?"

"And checking it twice."

"Okay. What's question number two?"

"Are you in love with him?"

Amy almost whispered the answer. "I am absolutely and totally in love with him."

"What makes you so sure? Your hormones or your heart?"

Amy didn't even have to think about how to answer that question. "My heart."

"Okay, question number three: 'If he betrayed you, would you still love him?'"

Amy hesitated, the painful memory of Daddy's betrayal clouding her mind. Finally, she spoke, her voice choking. "Yes. I would still love Ted if he betrayed me."

"So, you get an A, girl."

"Sara, don't joke with me."

"I'm not joking. If you love someone who betrays you, you love him with *agape* love, the only true kind of love. *Agape* love is based on the will, on a decision. All other kinds of love are based on feelings. And we both know that feelings can change from one minute to the next."

"Boy, do I know that! My feelings have been a Kingda Ka roller-coaster ride."

"A great adventure, huh! No pun intended."

Amy laughed at Sara's allusion to the world's largest roller coaster at the Great Adventure Amusement Park in New Jersey where they'd gone together the summer before.

Amy returned to the matter at hand. "So, you're okay with my marrying Ted?"

"It's not my decision, Amy. It's yours. But if you're asking if I think you're making the right one, I think you are. I think this is God's doing."

Amy's relief was palpable. "Thanks, Sara. I know you hear from the Lord, and I just needed a confirmation."

"Right on, girlfriend. The Bible says 'In the mouth of two or three witnesses shall every word be established.'"

"Where does it say that?"

"In 2 Corinthians 13: 1."

Amy chuckled. "Amen, then."

"Have you set a wedding date yet?"

"Not yet. But as soon as we do, I'll let you know."

Sara changed the subject. "So, how's the audit going?"

"It's almost finished. But I ran into some major problems."

"What kind of problems?"

"Embezzlement problems."

Sara gasped. "Are you serious?"

"Yes. Very serious." Amy paused. "So serious, in fact, that some people may be going to prison."

Sara released a low whistle. "Wow! That's pretty serious."

"I'll fill you in on the details when I get back."

"Sounds good. We'll catch up when I pick you up at the airport." Amy's heart warmed at Sara's loyalty.

"Thanks, Sara. We have a lot to catch up on. I want to hear about what's been happening in your life, too."

"It's been pretty much the same old, same old at headquarters. But, I'm not complaining. The same old, same old can be a good thing."

Amy pondered Sara's words. "Sara?"

"Yes?"

"Will you be my maid of honor?"

"Yahoo!" Sara's shout traveled across the line the full four thousand twenty-eight miles between New York and Milan in less than a second. "I sure will."

Amy laughed. "Thanks. When I get back, we'll go shopping for dresses."

"Sounds great!"

"Hey, Sara?"

"Yeah?"

"Thanks again."

"Any time, Amy."

Amy ended the call, the flicker of friendship lingering strong in her heart.

Chapter Thirteen

After leaving his Interpol meeting with Mr. Addevico, Ted texted Amy. "Can you meet me at the café' across the street from the office?"

Amy glanced at the time on her cell phone. Two-thirty p.m. She could take her coffee break now and work a little later tonight. "Sure. I'll be there in a few."

She logged off her computer, grabbed her shoulder bag, and headed to the little café across the street. It was one of her and Ted's favorite hangouts, a place away from the office where they could unwind and chat freely without interruption or observation. Plus, the coffee was great.

She exited the Enson building into the bright afternoon sunshine. The days were growing warmer in Italy as August got into full swing. Most of the city had left for the beaches. Only tourists crowded the squares. One could recognize them by the way their heads tilted upward as they marveled at the sights of this magnificent city.

Amy crossed the busy street, wending her way through crazy Italian drivers who didn't know the difference between the street and the sidewalk. The café was packed with tourists from all over the world. People of all nationalities, speaking in various languages. She loved the cosmopolitan feel of Italy. The country vibrated with life wherever she went. It would be difficult to leave this beautiful place.

She went straight to a table in the back where she and Ted usually sat. It was occupied. She looked around and found another table on the opposite end that sat a bit separate from the others. Perfect. She pulled out one of the two chairs and sat down to wait for Ted. Meanwhile, she checked her email on her cell phone.

"Hey."

Her heart jumped at the sound of Ted's deep, baritone voice. It sounded tired and concerned.

She looked up, warming all over. "Hey. What's up?"

He pulled out a chair and drew it up close to her. "I got some not-so-good news."

Her muscles tensed. "What happened?"

He proceeded to tell her about his meeting with Mr. Addevico. "Bottom line, I can't leave Italy until the case is over. And only if I'm found to be innocent."

Amy's heart sank to her feet. "When is the trial?"

"In a couple of months, if things go as they should. But if you think the American court system is slow, you should see the Italian court system. Italians seem to think there's always a tomorrow."

She studied the discouraged look on Ted's face and took his hands. "Ted, we'll get through this together."

He gave her a look of love that overwhelmed her. "Thanks. But you yourself said you have to remain unbiased in this investigation."

"I do—professionally, that is. But emotionally, I am far from unbiased. Emotionally, I'm entwined in it because my heart is entwined in yours."

He smiled weakly. "Well, you can't let that entwinement show. Or else, you, too, could go to jail."

She stiffened. "Who says you're going to jail? Stop thinking the worst. You're innocent, so you have nothing to fear."

"I wish I could be as confident as you. But you don't know Silvia. She'll do anything to malign me and to exonerate herself. In case you haven't noticed, Silvia is all about Silvia."

"I have noticed. But remember, Ted. God is in the business of miracles. If we ask Him to expose the truth, He will." She paused, her heart filling with tenderness. "Maybe He'll give us a miracle in Milan."

"A miracle in Milan." Ted smiled. "I like that."

She returned the smile. "Yes, a miracle in Milan. How's that for alliteration?"

He squeezed her hands. "Amy, you're the best thing that's ever happened to me. I don't know how I would get through this if you weren't by my side."

"You'd get through it because Jesus is by your side." Her words echoed in her own soul. Maybe she should take her own advice. Hadn't Jesus been by her side all of her life? Ever since she'd accepted Him as her Lord and Savior when but a child of seven years old? Hadn't He been by her side when Daddy abandoned her? And when she'd cried herself to sleep night after night for months afterward?

Truth was, Jesus had always been by her side. He'd never left her side.

But she'd left His.

A pang of guilt pierced her heart as tears welled up in her eyes. *Lord, can You ever forgive me for leaving your side?*

I already have, dear one.

She steadied her gaze on Ted. "Ted, listen to me. We're going to trust God for a miracle. We're going to expect Him to get you out of this mess so that we can both go back to Texas to serve Him."

Ted's eyes locked onto hers. "Amen and Amen."

* * * *

Silvia paced back and forth in the large solarium at Giorgio's country estate. She'd arrived earlier that afternoon to meet with Roberto Manero and his henchmen who now sat, watching her pace. A dark, gray sky portended a summer storm.

She stopped in front of Roberto. "I took care of changing all of my entries to make them look like Ted's."

Roberto smiled slyly. "Good. Now we have nothing to fear."

"But how can you be so sure? What if something backfires? What if things don't go according to plan?" She wrung her hands.

He smiled reassuringly. "Roberto Manero always has a contingency plan." He pointed to his men and then returned his gaze to Silvia. "I've been in this business long enough to know to cover all my bases."

"What are you saying?"

"I'm saying that if one method doesn't work, we always have another more effective one."

A chill ran through Silvia. "You're not considering murder, are you?"

He glared at her. "Nothing is beyond consideration."

She gasped. "Embezzlement is bad enough. I don't want to add murder to it."

"It's too late in the game, sweetheart. You should have thought of that sooner."

Remorse flooded her soul. What had she gotten herself into? As much as she wanted Ted to pay for rejecting her, she didn't want to go so far as to have him killed. She tried to stall Roberto. "Let's see what happens first. Once the authorities discover his identity next to my entries, they'll have all the evidence they need to send him to prison."

Roberto nodded. "Yes, that should be enough." He paused. "But, in case it isn't, we'll finish the job."

Silvia shivered. Better not to say anything more. Better to let things play out on their own.

Better never to have gotten herself into this mess.

* * * *

Amy returned from lunch early on Thursday afternoon. It was her last Thursday in Milan. The following Wednesday she'd be returning to the States. She had only a few days to prepare the final audit report for Mr. Conklin.

Back in the computer room, she sat in front of the big screen. A shaft of sunlight drifted through the window she'd opened to get some fresh air. The city had come alive. The sounds of early afternoon traffic filtered upward into the computer room, as did the clang and clatter of vendors selling their wares.

She needed to do one final check of the printout the computer technician had finally given her that morning of all the embedded usernames connected with each entry, just to make sure they were correct. This portion of the audit was the most critical since it defined who was responsible for posting each entry.

Amy zeroed in on the ledger entries before her, matching each entry with its embedded username. As she reviewed the fraudulent entries, her heart froze. Next to each one was Ted's username!

Impossible! Ted couldn't possibly be implicated with the embezzlement. There had to be some mistake.

She stared at each entry again and again, comparing it with the embedded username. It couldn't be. Amy double-checked and triple-checked the username. But there was no mistake about it. Ted's username was listed next to every fraudulent entry.

The blood drained from her veins as her world totally crashed. There was no mistake about it. Clearly, it appeared as though Ted was the embezzler.

She closed her eyes and swallowed a sob. Acid climbed to her throat, scalding it. He'd lied to her! Just as her father had lied to her. He'd betrayed her. Just as her father had betrayed her.

She rose from the desk and walked to the open window, choking in an attempt to catch her breath. How could she have been so stupid? So naïve? So blind? How could she not have seen the truth? How could she have allowed herself to fall for a man who was a criminal?

When would she ever learn?

The creak of the door startled her from her thoughts.

"Amy?"

The sound of Ted's voice made her stiffen. What could she say to him? There was nothing to say. Her heart was totally shattered.

Ted approached her. "I've been looking for you." He reached to take her hand.

She withdrew, as though he were a poisonous snake.

"What's the matter?"

She looked him squarely in the eye. "You lied to me, Ted."

His eyes widened. "What? What are you saying? I've never lied to you."

Why did men persist in their deceit, knowing full well they'd never get away with it?

She turned on him, all the fury buried within her now rising to the surface, like an erupting volcano. "You did so lie to me! And I have proof!"

He took her by the arms. "Amy, listen to me. I don't know what you're talking about. Would you please explain?"

"Yes. I'll explain. I'll show you."

She showed him the printout. "The computer technician gave me this. I've been matching the usernames with the entries. Look whose username is next to every single fraudulent entry." Amy pointed to the username.

"It's mine." His voice was low.

"Yes. Yours! So, what do you have to say for yourself now, Ted McMasters?"

"I didn't make those entries."

"But your username is next to each one and shows that you did."

"I tell you I didn't make them."

"Then who did? Mickey Mouse?" The sarcasm in her voice sliced the air between them.

"Somebody changed the username."

"But how? You don't know one another's usernames."

Ted sat down, a worried look on his face. But why was he worried? Was it that he was guilty and had been caught red-handed?

"Let's pray."

"I don't want to pray. I have enough evidence to know that I'm a fool for falling in love with you."

"Amy, please." A pained look crossed his face.

If he betrayed you, would you still love him? Sara's question flooded back into her mind.

"Ted, I'm sorry. It's just that I am so hurt. You were the first man I ever loved and chose to trust since my father left me. You have no idea what choosing to give you my trust meant to me. And now, just like my father, you've gone and betrayed that trust."

"But, Amy. I'm telling you the truth."

She faced him, tears rolling down her cheeks. "I'm sorry, Ted. I don't believe you. The evidence to the contrary is so overwhelming." She stifled a sob. "Now, please leave. I have nothing more to say to you."

He rose, his eyes glistening. "Okay. If that's what you want."

"It's what I want."

He turned and left, quietly shutting the door behind him.

Amy laid her head against the table and sobbed and sobbed and sobbed. If only there were some way to prove that the computer data was wrong.

But that would take a miracle.

Chapter Fourteen

Amy's accusation hit Ted like a bombshell. Seated at his desk in his office, he wracked his brain until he could think no more. Someone had gotten a hold of his username. But who? And how? And why? Now, as a result, he could be found guilty of a crime he didn't commit.

His heart ached. Not only had Interpol questioned his integrity, but, worst of all, Amy had questioned it. And Amy was the only one whose opinion really mattered to him.

He bowed his head and prayed. "Lord, You know who did this evil thing. Please expose the truth. And please restore Amy's trust in me."

* * * *

The digital clock in Amy's hotel room read five-thirty a.m., Friday morning. She'd been tossing and turning in her bed all night, trying desperately to discover a loophole in her findings regarding Ted's guilt. But she could find nothing.

Check after check after check had revealed the same thing: Ted's username was connected to all of the fraudulent entries. No amount of rationalization could change that. She'd do well to resign herself to the fact that she'd fallen in love with an embezzler. A criminal.

A traitor.

Yes, a traitor. That was the worst of it. The most painful part. Ted had lied to her. She could overlook almost any flaw, but a flaw in integrity she could never overlook.

She released the sobs that had been building in her throat. Her pillow was already drenched with bitter tears. Would she ever stop crying? Could she ever stop crying?

Yes. One day she'd stop crying. The way she'd stopped crying whenever she thought about her father. One day, her heart would dry up again. And this time, she'd keep her promise to herself never to allow any man to water it again.

Never!

Amy's attempt to sleep was futile. She got up to make herself a cup of chamomile tea. Perhaps it would calm her shattered nerves.

As the tea water heated, she noticed her wristwatch on the kitchenette counter. She'd removed it from her wrist the evening before when she was getting ready for bed. Suddenly, she remembered Ted's watch and shouted. "Tracker watch! That could be the answer! Ted's tracker watch!"

Ted's smart wristwatch could provide the proof of his innocence because it recorded everywhere he'd been and the time he'd been there. All she had to do was match his tracker watch data with the ledger time stamp, and, if he were really innocent, she could prove that Ted did not make the fraudulent entries.

She was so excited she had to call Ted, even though it was early in the morning.

Taking her tea into the living room, she sat down on the couch and tapped on his number.

"Hey!" Ted's groggy voice made her heart soar.

"Ted, I'm so sorry to wake you up so early, but I just had an amazing idea that could prove you're innocent."

"Shoot!"

"Your tracker watch!"

"My tracker watch?"

"Yes. You told me that it records where you've been and when you've been there."

"Right."

"Well, all we have to do is compare the time stamp on the ledger entries with the time stamp on your tracker watch. Your watch will show where you were at the time the entries were made and could prove your innocence."

Ted cleared his throat. "Praise the Lord! That's a miracle!"

Time stood still as Amy pondered Ted's words. God had not forsaken her after all. He'd been true and faithful. He'd kept His Word to be a good Father to her.

Amy's heart filled to overflowing. Suddenly everything became clear. People would fail her, but God would never fail her. She could stake her life on His faithfulness. And that's all she needed in order to make it.

"Yes, Ted. God gave us our miracle in Milan."

"What do you say we go to the office early and compare the ledger with my tracker watch?"

Amy agreed.

"I'll pick you up in an hour."

"Okay."

"And Amy?"

"Yes, Ted?"

"I love you, and I always will."

"I love you, too, Ted."

* * * *

Dawn had just begun to extend her rosy fingers across the sky when Ted picked Amy up at six-thirty a.m. The air was already warm, portending an especially hot day.

Amy slid into the passenger seat of Ted's Fiat. She never thought she'd ride in his car with him again.

As he drove to the Enson office, he turned toward her. "I'm still reeling from what the Lord showed you. I had been fervently praying He would provide a way out."

"Well, He certainly did. He said He is the Way, the Truth, and the Life." She told him about her wristwatch on the kitchenette counter and how it had triggered the thought about his tracker watch.

"That was the Lord for sure. He showed you the connection."

She laughed. "So, you did bring your watch with you, didn't you?"

He raised his left arm from the steering wheel. "It's right here on my wrist."

Amy smiled at the sight of the smartwatch, eager to compare its time stamps with the ledger entries.

When they reached the Enson building, dawn had given way to a bright day. Ted unlocked the door of the building and Amy accompanied him to the computer room.

Her heart pounded as she looked at the computer screen. She found the first entry made out to RobMan Enterprises and noted the date. "It's marked February 13, 7:38 p.m."

Ted found the same date on his tracker watch. "Here's February 13th. The record says I was in Torino for an indoor tennis match and didn't get back to Milan until 10: 31 p.m."

Amy's heart soared. "There's our proof. Now let's check all of the fraudulent entries."

One by one, Amy scrolled to each entry and compared the date and time recorded on the screen with Ted's tracker watch record. The tracker watch proved that Ted was elsewhere at the time every single fraudulent entry was made.

Amy turned toward Ted. "I have to get this information to Mr. Addevico right away. I'll call him and tell him we're on our way."

"But it's only seven-thirty."

"Then let's grab a coffee and a *brioche* along the way."

Ted smiled. "Great idea!"

"But first I want to print out the ledger with all the dates and times of entry in case Mr. Addevico doesn't have his copy readily available."

Amy quickly printed out a copy of the ledger and tucked it

under her arm together with the computer technician's report. Then she turned to Ted. "Let's go before any of the employees arrive for work. I don't want them finding us here together before hours."

She logged off and shut down the computer. With Ted close at her side, she hastened down the corridor leading to the parking lot. But just as they reached the door, it opened. In walked Silvia, accompanied by a man Amy did not recognize.

"Well, good morning!" Silvia cooed. "What a pleasant surprise to find you two here so early."

Amy's muscles tensed.

Ted took the lead in responding. "The surprise is mutual."

Silvia gave him a smile. "I'd like you both to meet a good friend of mine, Mr. Roberto Manero. He has an early appointment with Giorgio."

Amy froze. Her gaze flew to Ted. Was their miracle in Milan about to turn into a nightmare?

She'd play it cool. She extended her hand. "A pleasure to meet you, Mr. Manero. I seem to have seen your name somewhere." She didn't tell him she'd seen it on the ledger. And on the Internet as she'd researched him.

He chuckled. "Probably in a newspaper headline."

Amy played dumb. Mr. Conklin would be proud of her. "Oh, so I am speaking with a celebrity?"

Manero laughed. "Of sorts."

"And a humble one at that." Amy wasn't flattering, just being wise as a serpent. "I will have to look up your accomplishments, Mr. Manero. I'm sure they are many."

Silvia jumped in. "So, you are leaving?"

"Yes. But we'll be back. We're just going out to grab a cup of coffee."

"With papers under your arm?"

Amy looked down at the papers she held tightly under her

arm. "Uh . . . " She stuttered. "Yes. I'm going to work on them at home. I'm on a tight deadline since I return to the States next week and need to take advantage of every moment."

Silvia gave Roberto a sidelong glance.

Amy smiled. "Well, it was nice to meet you, Mr. Manero. Perhaps we'll see each other again before I leave. If not, I wish you the best." Amy turned to Ted. "We'd better get going. Time waits for no man."

And with that, she and Ted left.

Chapter Fifteen

"Well, that was a close call." Ted's voice echoed at her side.

Amy shuddered. "Yes, too close for comfort."

"Do you think Silvia recognized the copy of the ledger under your arm?"

"I don't know. If she did, too bad."

Ted turned toward her. "The guy with her, you remember who he was, don't you?"

"Yes. The top Mafioso of Milan."

"You got that right," Ted said. "You did a good job at playing dumb."

Amy laughed. "Thanks. That's Mr. Conklin's doing. He gave me a crash course before I left. Said I needed to be as wise as a serpent, but as gentle as a dove."

"I'll tell him to give you a promotion for your great acting skills."

Amy laughed and hopped into Ted's car, placing the ledger and the technician's report on her lap. "Mr. Addevico will be surprised to see this. He can now compare the date and time stamps on the ledger with the date and time stamps on your tracker watch. The comparison will prove that you could not possibly have made the entries because you were elsewhere when the entries were made."

Just after eight a.m., Ted pulled his car into a parking spot in front of the Interpol office. Eager to give Mr. Addevico the updated report, Amy didn't wait for Ted to open the door for her but let herself out. "I can't wait to see the look on his face."

"Neither can I."

"And I can't wait to see you exonerated." More than anything else, she wanted Ted to be proven innocent. She needed him to be proven innocent.

Mr. Addevico was in a staff meeting when they arrived, but his secretary said it would be over soon. After a brief ten-minute wait, she ushered them into his office.

"Well, well, well. To what do I owe your visit? I hope it's good news."

Amy spoke first. "It's very good news, Mr. Addevico. At least, we think so."

He offered them seats in his private office.

Amy handed him the ledger and the technician's report. "Here is a copy of the ledger that I printed out just before I came, in case you didn't have yours handy. I also brought a copy of the computer technician's report that reveals the data embedded on the hard drive."

Mr. Addevico pointed to a large table behind them. "Let's go over to the conference table where we can spread things out." He opened the documents and placed them side-by-side on the large conference table. "Okay. Let's take a look. Show me what you want me to see."

Amy pointed to one of the fraudulent entries on the ledger: RobMan Enterprises, February 13, 7:38 p.m. She then pointed to that same entry on the technician's report and turned to Mr. Addevico. "Notice that the technician's report seems to prove that Ted made the fraudulent entries. But we can prove that he didn't."

Mr. Addevico arched his eyebrows. "Really? How?"

Ted smiled and raised his left wrist.

Mr. Addevico gave him a questioning look. "*Non capisco.* I don't understand."

Amy jumped in. "His tracker watch."

A puzzled look crossed Mr. Addevico's face. "Tracker watch?"

"Yes. Ted's smartwatch. It's a device that records not only his location throughout the day but also the precise time he was at each location."

Mr. Addevico grew curious. "May I take a look?"

Ted removed his tracker watch from his wrist and showed Mr. Addevico the data proving he was in Torino at an indoor tennis match at 7:38 p.m. on the night of February 13th.

"Amazing!" Mr. Addevico took note.

Amy smiled. "And the same is true of all of the fraudulent entries. So, we now have proof of Ted's innocence in the embezzlement."

"It certainly seems that way. We will need to present this evidence in court. Ted, is there a way to print out the record on your tracker watch?"

"I can retrieve the data from my online account. I'll do that and email the file to you as soon as I get back to the office."

"Yes, please do." Mr. Addevico smiled. "This information will, I believe, if it holds up in court, exonerate you from any and all guilt. But it remains for the court to decide that."

Ted nodded.

Amy tensed. "But surely the court won't be able to deny the facts."

Mr. Addevico looked at her. "My gut feeling is no. But I've been in this business long enough to know that anything can go wrong at any time."

Amy's stomach clenched. She couldn't' bear another thing going wrong. Worst of all, she couldn't bear leaving Italy with the thought that Ted might still be put behind bars.

And for a crime he didn't commit.

* * * *

Silvia rubbed her finger around the rim of her coffee cup as she sat with Roberto Manero in the Enson cafeteria. Her mind had zeroed in on the papers Amy held under her arm when they'd run into each other that morning. The papers had to be a copy of the ledger.

Roberto leaned forward. "So, you think Amy and Ted are up to no good?"

"Of course. From the moment she arrived from the States, Amy Torelli was up to no good."

Roberto leaned back in his chair. "Well, I guess it depends on whose perspective you take. Anyone whose job is to uncover an embezzlement is up to no good from the embezzler's point of view but not from the honest person's point of view."

Silva smirked. "You think you're funny, don't you, Roberto?"

"A little humor in the midst of big trouble never hurt."

She grew serious. "Do you think we're in big trouble?"

"Well, I wouldn't call this a stroll in the park. Amy has discovered there's an embezzler in the house, and now she needs to discover who that embezzler is."

Silvia wrung her hands. "And I fear she's getting pretty close to finding out."

"I think she already knows."

Roberto's words took Silvia aback. "Then where does that leave us?"

"It depends on how we play the game."

Silvia furrowed her brows. "What do you mean?"

"We have tools Miss Torelli doesn't have."

"Like what?"

Roberto smiled slyly. "Like hit men and bribes."

"You wouldn't dare!"

"Why not? We dared embezzlement."

For the first time in a long time, Silvia's seared conscience came to life. She remembered the words of an old priest: *Silvia, always tell the truth and shame the devil.* It seemed as though the devil now sat right in front of her in the person of Roberto Manero.

"I want no parts of your dirty schemes, Roberto."

"Sorry, Silvia. As I told you before, it's too late. You're already embroiled in them. There's no backing out now."

She started to open her mouth to protest but then thought the better of it. Whatever scheme she devised, she would do well to keep it to herself.

* * * *

Providing the tracker watch info to Mr. Addevico had given Ted renewed hope for his acquittal as a suspect in the embezzlement case. He turned toward Amy, sitting beside him in his tiny Fiat. She'd become a welcome fixture there. Her presence beside him felt so natural. So normal. So good. He imagined having her by his side for the rest of his life.

He turned toward her. "You know, if it weren't for you, I'd still be a serious suspect in this case."

She smiled. "We have the Lord to thank. He's the One Who reminded me of your tracker watch."

"Yes. He deserves all the glory. I'm so glad He brought my smartwatch to your mind."

"I am, too. I'd hate to have to return to New York on Wednesday worrying you had no chance in the court case."

His voice mellowed. "Speaking of Wednesday, this is your last weekend in Milan. I'd like us to make the most of it."

Amy's voice hitched. "Yes. I know. I've been thinking about that a lot."

"Let's do something special."

"What do you have in mind?"

"I was thinking we could take a drive to Lake Como tomorrow and spend the day there. We could have lunch by the lake and then be back by tomorrow night so we could go to church together on Sunday morning."

Amy looked at Ted. "How far is Lake Como from Milan?"

"Only about 85 kilometers." Ted laughed. "Or 50 miles to a fellow Texan. It's the perfect distance for a day trip."

"It sounds awesome. Let's do it."

Ted took her hand, a lump forming in his throat. "Amy, I'm really going to miss you."

"I'm going to miss you, too, Ted."

He glanced at her. "I was hoping I could hand in my resignation and return to the States shortly after you do. But with the case now pending, it looks as though I'm going to have to stay here for several more months."

"I hope it's not that long. Maybe now that your watch proves your innocence, you won't have to stay around at all."

"That would be another miracle, wouldn't it?"

"Who says God wants to give us only one?"

Ted smiled. "I love your faith."

"I wish I were the faith giant you think I am."

He pondered her words. "You know, when we truly get to know God, we discover that He is perfectly trustworthy, no matter what the situation."

"Yes. The problem is that most of us take a long time to get to know God, if we get to know Him at all."

Ted pulled into the parking lot of the Enson building. "I hope we don't run into Silvia and Roberto again."

"I hear you. I'm troubled that they saw us leaving this morning. Silvia isn't the nicest person on earth and Roberto—Well, I put nothing past him." Amy's voice sounded worried. "You don't think he has anything up his sleeve, do you?"

Ted patted her hand. "I wouldn't worry about it. We just got done saying that God is trustworthy, didn't we?"

Amy nodded.

"So, let's trust Him to take care of us."

"Yes. That's all we can do." She turned toward him. "Ted, please be careful, nonetheless."

"I will." He looked at her. "And you, too."

"I will."

Chapter Sixteen

Once back at the office, Amy grabbed a bite of lunch and went straight to the computer room. She had a few more things to wrap up as she prepared the final report for Mr. Conklin. With only two more workdays left in the Italian office the following week, she wanted to be sure she didn't miss anything.

As she sat in front of the computer, she had a hard time concentrating. The thought of leaving Ted ate at her. Worst of all, the thought of leaving him alone in the pack of ravenous wolves that hid in Enson's Milan office gave her pause.

Should she ask Mr. Conklin for an extension to stay? Even if he granted it to her, what good would that do? She hadn't been required to appear in person in the upcoming court case. Her report would provide sufficient evidence for the defense. So, staying behind made no sense. Besides, she was needed back in the New York office. During her time away, her routine work had suffered. She'd have a lot to catch up on upon her return.

Her mind drifted back to her and Ted's unfortunate encounter with Silvia and Roberto earlier that morning. The two of them were up to no good. Amy sensed it in her bones. A rush of uneasiness swept over her. Her mind imagined all the horrible things they could do to Ted to get Silvia off the hook. Amy wasn't too worried about Giorgio. For all of his wicked ways, he didn't seem like the type to resort to drastic measures against Ted. But, Roberto? She wouldn't put anything past him.

Amy startled at the click of the door opening behind her. She turned. "Hello, Silvia." Amy forced a smile.

"Oh. I'm sorry. I thought the computer was free."

"It will be in a few moments. Is there anything I can do for you?"

"I just need to print out a copy of last month's ledger."

Amy went on high alert. "Oh? All the reports have been printed out and already submitted to Interpol."

Silvia hesitated. "Giorgio has requested a copy."

"But I already gave him one."

Silvia averted her gaze. "He must have misplaced it."

Was this a ruse? There was no reason Silvia or Giorgio would need a copy of last month's ledger unless they wanted to alter something. And that would have to be done on the computer itself.

Amy smiled. "I'll be happy to print out a copy for you."

"No. That won't be necessary. I'll just wait until you're finished."

Amy pretended to go along with her so as not to arouse her suspicion. "Okay. I'll be finished in about ten minutes. I'll text you when the computer is free."

"Very good."

After Silvia left, Amy texted Mr. Addevico to inquire what to do about Silvia's request.

"No worries," Mr. Addevico texted back. "Anything she changes now will make no difference since Ted just emailed me his tracker watch log."

Relief flooded Amy. She and Ted were good to go.

Or, so she hoped, as she texted Silvia to tell her the computer was now available.

* * * *

Saturday dawned beautiful and bright, one of the loveliest days so far during Amy's entire stay in Italy. Anticipating a fun time with Ted, she showered and dressed in preparation for the special outing with him to Lake Como. Mixed feelings conflicted her heart. Joy at spending the day with the man she loved, and sorrow at having to leave him soon. She decided to focus on the joy, on living in the moment, and not worrying about the future.

Ted was waiting for her in the hotel lobby at seven o'clock sharp.

She greeted him with a warm hug. "Great day for a trek to Lake Como!"

Ted took her hand and gave her his brilliant Texas smile. "Any day's a great day to be with you."

Heat rose to Amy's face. She'd never thought she could ever be this happy again.

They made their way to Ted's car parked outside the hotel. Tourists were out in full force, starting their day with a light breakfast at one of the many outdoor cafés before scouring the lovely boutiques for bargains and more. Today was especially busy as it was the height of the tourist season.

Amy would miss the hustle and bustle of this magnificent city. The city that, over the past three weeks, had totally transformed her life.

She buckled her seatbelt as Ted pulled out of the parking spot in front of the hotel and made his way to the *Autostrada dei Laghi*, the Highway of the Lakes, leading north out of Milan toward Lake Como.

He glanced at her. "Are you excited?"

"Very."

"You'll love *Lago di Como*. It's one of the most beautiful spots in Italy and a great place to vacation." He glanced at her and took her hand. "Maybe one day, after we're married, we can come back to vacation there."

"That would be awesome." She settled into her seat, the thought of being married to Ted filling her heart with joy.

"Speaking of marriage, don't you think we should set a wedding date?"

"I guess so. With everything that's been going on, and with so many things up in the air, I haven't really thought much about a date."

Ted looked alarmed. "You haven't changed your mind, have you?"

"Not since the tracker watch discovery." She paused. "But, to be honest with you, when I first saw your ID next to the Manero entries, I was ready to break our engagement."

He let out a long sigh of relief. "I owe my life to my tracker watch. Maybe I should buy us some stock in the company."

Amy laughed. "That's a great idea."

They reached Lake Como about ninety minutes later. Ted parked the car in a small parking area. "Are you ready?"

"Ready." Amy scanned the lovely lake before her. The morning sunshine cast a shimmering swath of light across the water, beckoning her toward it. The surrounding mountains, green with lush foliage, glimmered in the sunshine, while banks of brilliant pansies and marigolds lined a retaining wall along the shore.

Ted held her hand tightly. "Let's walk along the shore to get the feel of the place. Then we can decide if we want to go hiking or boating or both."

"Sounds good."

Hand in hand, they strolled around the lake. Amy took in the beautiful views, the fragrance of the blossoming flowers, and the warm breeze that drifted across the water.

She spoke first. "So, Silvia came into the computer room yesterday, wanting to print out a copy of the ledger."

"Oh, really?"

"I offered to do it for her, but she insisted on returning to do it herself when the computer was available."

"So, what did you do?"

"I called Mr. Addevico to ask him what to do. He said not to worry. The reports he had from your tracker watch would take care of any problem Silvia might create."

"Then there's nothing to worry about."

"That's what Mr. Addevico said. But why do I have this uneasy feeling that the bottom is about to fall out of this whole thing?"

Ted stopped and took her gently by the shoulders. "Let's just enjoy our day together and trust God to take care of everything." He gave her a peck on the forehead.

Amy nodded. "Yes. You're right. I guess I just have a wild imagination. Too wild for my own good."

The day passed by quickly, with a fun hike through the hills and a peaceful boat ride across the lake and back. By the time evening came, Amy was hungry.

"Are you up for a pizza?" Ted asked as he helped her out of the boat.

"Yes. I'm famished."

They found a charming little pizzeria along the edge of the water and ordered a *pizza Margherita*. As her eyes drank in the beauty of the lake, Amy wished she could hold this moment in time forever. Ted's presence beside her, the brilliant setting sun washing over the water, the sound of a mandolinist playing a haunting, Italian love song—she wanted to capture the precious moment forever in her heart.

As the waiter came to check on their table, Amy's gaze shifted to the other people in the pizzeria. Her heart stopped at the sight of Roberto Manero, staring at her from a table across the room.

* * * *

"Ted! Don't look, but Roberto Manero is sitting across the room, staring at us."

"Are you sure it's he, or just someone who looks like him?"

"I'm sure. I'd recognize him anywhere. There's a sinister look about him." Amy's heart raced. "What shall we do?"

"Nothing. Pretend you don't see him."

Amy tensed. "He's already caught my eye." She kept her gaze fixed on Ted. "How did he know we'd be at Lake Como today?"

"I have no idea. He's probably stalking us."

Amy lowered her voice. "Should we call Mr. Addevico?"

"Yes."

Amy reached for her phone but discovered it was dead. "Oh, no! My battery ran out. May I borrow your phone? I know his personal cell number."

Ted surreptitiously slid his phone toward Amy. "How can you call him without being noticed?"

"I'll text him instead."

"You'll have to be really discreet since Manero has his eyes trained on us."

"Maybe I should go to the restroom to call him. It's on this side of the restaurant."

Ted agreed. "That's a good idea."

Her body trembling, Amy slipped Ted's phone into her shoulder bag, rose, and made her way to the restroom. Once there, she quickly dialed Mr. Addevico's number.

"Salvatore here."

"Mr. Addevico, thank God you answered. This is Amy Torelli." She quickly explained what was happening and told him where they were.

"Stay right where you are. Do not leave the restaurant. I'll have men there shortly."

"Thank you so much." She replaced Ted's cell phone in her shoulder bag and returned to the table.

But her heart froze. Ted was gone!

Chapter Seventeen

Amy frantically looked around. Not only was Ted missing, but Roberto was also. Panic lodged in her throat. What should she do?

She sat down at the table to gather her thoughts. She'd have to stay because the Interpol police were on their way. But meanwhile, she'd ask the waiter if he'd seen Ted leave.

She searched for her waiter and found him at the back of the restaurant. "Did you happen to see my *fiancé* leave?"

The waiter looked at her questioningly.

"The man I was with? Did you see him leave?"

"Ah." Understanding lit the waiter's face. "*Sì.* He left suddenly with some men who came over to your table. I thought it strange, but I don't intervene in customer's affairs."

"Thank you. You've been a big help. Did my friend pay the bill?"

"No, ma'am."

Amy took enough from her wallet to cover the meal and the tip and handed it to the waiter.

"*Grazie.*"

She then threw her shoulder bag over her shoulder and went to the entrance of the pizzeria to await Interpol.

In a few moments, two men appeared at the entrance to the restaurant and approached the hostess. Amy overheard one of them say they were looking for an Amy Torelli.

Amy rushed toward them. "I'm Amy Torelli."

The two men showed her their ID cards from Interpol.

"Thank God you're here!" The words rushed out of Amy's mouth. "My fiancé has disappeared. I was in the ladies' room calling Mr. Addevico and returned to find him gone. The waiter said he saw him leave with some other men. One of them was Roberto Manero."

The two Interpol officers looked at each other.

One of the officers asked, "Does your *fiancé* have a cell phone? Maybe we could track him down that way."

"I have his phone here. But he wears a tracker watch. There's an app on his phone that can locate the watch."

"Great! We can use it to locate where the men took him."

Amy handed Ted's phone to one of the officers and showed him the tracker watch app. The other officer then asked her if she had a way of getting home.

"Ted's car should still be here, but I don't have his keys."

"Okay. Stay here for now. We'll get someone to take you home. Then stay there until further notice. Do not communicate with anyone other than your *fiancé* or Interpol. Is that clear?"

Amy nodded emphatically. "Yes. It's clear."

Within a half hour, a female officer from the local Interpol office appeared and drove Amy back to her hotel. Once there, the first thing Amy did was to plug in her cell phone to charge it. Then she fell to her knees beside the bed. "God, I need You now more than I've ever needed You. I'm frantic with fear about Ted. I don't know what's happened to him, but You do. Father, protect him from all evil. Bring him back safely to me. I pray in the Name of Jesus. Amen."

* * * *

The strong hand of one of Manero's henchman held Ted tightly by his shirt collar and pushed him forward along what seemed like a dirt road beneath Ted's feet. The man had tied Ted's hands behind his back and blindfolded him so that Ted would have no idea of his location. But since they hadn't gotten into a car, Ted figured they were somewhere local.

They entered a building of some sort and the man slammed the door behind him. After a few moments, he pushed Ted forcefully into a chair. "Now talk!"

"What do you want me to say?"

"What does Interpol know about the embezzlement?"

"They know that I'm innocent."

The man slapped Ted across the face.

Ted smarted at the sudden burning sensation.

"Does Interpol know about Manero?"

Ted remained silent. All he knew was what he and Amy had told Interpol, but he did not know the full extent of Interpol's knowledge.

The man slapped him again. "Answer my question!"

"I don't know what Interpol knows."

"Don't mess with Roberto Manero's men, you hear?"

"I'm not trying to mess with you. I'm trying only to answer your questions."

The man laughed. "So, you're a wise guy, eh?" The man slapped Ted a third time, this time more forcefully. The sensation of blood dripping into his mouth unnerved him. He prayed a silent prayer. *Father, deliver me from this nightmare. Protect Amy, wherever she is.*

The sound of multiple voices told Ted there were several men present. Roberto Manero's voice rose above the others. "If he keeps giving you lip, you know what to do with him."

Ted panicked. Manero was known to be ruthless when it came to killing anyone who got in his way. Suddenly, Ted's whole life flashed before him. What had he done with his life? Not much. And, truth be told, he'd done nothing for the Lord. All of his accomplishments had been for himself. For his glory alone and not the Lord's.

A pang of remorse swept over him. *Lord, if I were to meet you tonight—as well I might—I have nothing to show for the life*

You've given me. Please forgive me. If You give me a second chance, I promise You I'll live the rest of my life for You.

Suddenly, conviction about his father overwhelmed him. He'd never truly forgiven his father. Instead, he'd harbored anger, hatred, and resentment toward him. If Ted were to die tonight, he'd die in unforgiveness. How could he then expect God to forgive him?

He swallowed hard. "Lord," he whispered under his breath, "I forgive my father. I release his debt against me. I let go of all ill will toward him."

Now, I can forgive you, My Son.

Deep peace settled over Ted.

Just then, a sudden commotion disrupted the room. A loud voice rose above the chatter. "Stand back! Interpol here. Any move and you're dead."

Ted breathed a long sigh of relief as the pent-up tension unleashed itself from his body and soul. Tears of gratitude stung his eyes.

In a few seconds, an Interpol officer removed the blindfold from Ted's eyes and untied his hands.

"Whew! Thanks! It feels so good to be free."

The officer smiled. "That was a close call, my friend. Glad we got here before they finished you off—thanks to your tracker watch app." The officer returned Ted's phone to him.

"So am I." He shook his head and sighed. "Believe me. So am I!"

"You have a cut on your lip. Do you want some medical attention?"

"No. I just want to get back to my fiancée, wherever she is."

"We had her taken back to her hotel in Milan."

Ted breathed a sigh of relief. "Thanks!"

The remaining four Interpol officers handcuffed Manero and

his men and took them away. The officer who'd released Ted looked at him. "Do you have a way home?"

"Yes. I have my car."

"I'll drive you to it." The officer pointed to Ted's lip. "Are you sure you're okay to drive home?"

"Yes. I'm okay."

Once Ted reached his car, he unlocked it and then thanked the officer again for saving his life.

The officer smiled. "It's all in a day's work, my friend. All in a day's work."

"Well, I'm glad you're the one with this job and not me."

The officer chuckled. "It's all about the work God calls us to."

Ted grew serious. "Yes. That's all that matters." He gave the officer a firm handshake. "God bless you, man!"

"God bless you, too."

For the first time in Ted's life, those words had new meaning.

* * * *

The night wore on in Amy's hotel room as she prayed for Ted, on her knees, crying out to God on Ted's behalf. Would God hear her after she'd neglected Him for so many years? She had no claim on His mercy. Why would He give her any now?

She tensed. Somewhere out there, Ted, the man she loved and planned to marry, was either alive or dead. Her heart ached with worry.

The Interpol officer had told her to stay put until she heard from Ted or them. But staying put was becoming impossible. Mama used to say that no news was good news, but if Amy didn't get some news soon—any news—she'd lose her mind. It was already ten p.m. Three hours of waiting, worrying over Ted's safety, were about to drive her stir crazy.

She wanted so much to call Sara but didn't dare to tie up the phone line. Maybe a cup of hot coffee would calm her shattered nerves.

She walked over to the coffee pot in the kitchenette area of the hotel room. As she poured herself a cup of coffee, her cell phone rang. Startled by the ring, she nearly dropped the coffee pot.

She ran to grab her cell phone. It was Ted. Her knees buckled beneath her as she made her way to the nearest chair. "Ted! Where are you?" She burst into tears as relief flooded her soul.

"I'm okay. I'm on my way back to Milan. I'm just leaving Lake Como." He then told her all that had transpired. How he'd been abducted from the pizzeria with a threat from Manero to kill her. How he'd been tied up and blindfolded. Taken to an unknown location somewhere along the lake. How God had sent the Interpol police to rescue him after they'd tracked him down using his tracker watch. "That watch has saved my life twice. Good thing you used my cell phone to make the call to Mr. Addevico."

"Yes, but if I hadn't left you alone and gone to the restroom, you might never have been abducted."

"Or both of us might have been abducted."

Ted was probably right. "I hadn't thought of that." She breathed a sigh of relief. "You have no idea how glad I am to hear your voice. I was afraid they might kill you. I prayed for you the whole time." She choked back a sob. "And you know what? God heard my prayer."

"Why wouldn't He hear your prayer, sweetheart?"

"Because I don't deserve His mercy."

"None of us deserves His mercy, Amy. But He gives it to us anyway when we ask."

Ted's words penetrated her heart. "When Daddy left, I began a downward spiral away from God. I virtually turned my back on Him. It took you to bring me to my senses."

"Why, thank you." Ted chuckled. "But I didn't plan to do it in such a dramatic way." He paused. "Speaking of your father, Amy, have you decided to forgive him?"

She hesitated. If she were honest with herself, she hadn't. "No. I don't think I can forgive him for what he did to Mama and me."

"You know, Amy, Scripture says that if we don't forgive those who have hurt us, God won't forgive us. That's a pretty sobering thought, don't you think?"

Amy shuddered. Was she willing to take such a risk?

Ted continued. "While I was a hostage tonight, I didn't know if I would make it. I cried out to God and He reminded me that I needed to forgive my dad. So, I did."

"But how?"

"Forgiveness is not a feeling, Amy. It's a decision."

She turned Ted's words over and over in her mind. "You mean I can just choose to forgive, regardless of how I feel?"

"Yes. It's that simple."

She hesitated.

"Tomorrow is promised to no one, Amy."

Ted was right. She needed to forgive her father.

Ted changed the subject. "Hey, are you up for a late-night snack? My ordeal used up all of my pizza calories and stirred up quite an appetite."

Amy laughed. How she loved this man who made the worst situation seem like a picnic! "Yes, I'd love a late-night snack."

"Okay. I should be back in Milan in about an hour and a half. I'll call you from the lobby when I get there. If the hotel restaurant is open, we can grab something there."

"Sounds good. It's an all-night restaurant."

"I love you, Amy Torelli." There was a tone in Ted's voice that sprang from a new depth of gratitude for life and for love.

"I love you, too, Ted McMasters."

Amy ended the call and fell to her knees yet again. The

memory of her father's betrayal tore into her gut. Suddenly, in her mind's eye, she saw Jesus hanging on the Cross. Marred and disfigured beyond recognition. Covered with blood. She saw the nails in His hands and feet. She saw the gape in His side where the sword had pierced Him. Overcome with emotion, she began to weep. Mustering all the courage within her, she cried out, "Lord, help me to forgive my father. I want to, but I need Your help."

My grace is sufficient for you, dear one.

As the tears flowed, peace filled Amy's heart. She rose from her knees with the feeling that her life was just about to begin.

Chapter Eighteen

Wednesday morning found Ted with a painful gape in his stomach. Today Amy would be returning to the States. When would he see her again? The court case had yet to be scheduled, and only God knew how long it would be before the case began, let alone ended. He'd hoped to join her back in the States in the near future, but that hope had been shattered. For all he knew, he could be stuck in Italy for months, maybe even years. Mr. Conklin had graciously decided to keep Ted on the payroll until after the case.

Despite the tracker watch evidence proving his innocence, Ted had been ordered by Enson attorneys to remain in Italy for the court case. It had something to do with legal protocol. But it made no sense to him.

He glanced at the wall clock in his apartment. Seven o'clock a.m. He'd arranged to meet Amy at her hotel at seven-thirty and take her to the airport for her ten o'clock flight to New York. If time permitted, they'd share a last cup of espresso in the same airport where they'd first met.

Ted swallowed hard. The thought of her leaving made him feel as though he were losing a limb. He went to his dresser drawer and withdrew a little black velvet box containing the engagement ring for Amy he'd purchased the day before. He opened the lid and looked at the brilliant diamond ring that sat in the box. Yes, she'd agreed to marry him, but he hadn't yet given her a ring. He'd give it to her at the airport, just before she boarded the plane.

A lump rose to his throat as he anticipated her reaction. One day soon, Lord willing, he'd join her in the States. One day soon, Lord willing, she'd become his bride. One day soon, Lord willing, they'd move to the little Texas town where a tiny church needed a pastor.

One day soon.

He grabbed his car keys and headed for Amy's hotel. He found her waiting in the lobby, with two suitcases by her side. "Are you ready?"

Tears glistened in her lovely hazel eyes. "No."

He gazed into her eyes. "Neither am I."

A valet came up to them. "Do you need help with your bags?"

Ted intervened. "No, thanks. I've got them." He carried both suitcases to his car and helped Amy get in.

They rode to the airport, Ted's heart breaking within him. "Will Sara be picking you up at the airport?"

"Yes." Amy's voice quivered.

"I'm looking forward to meeting her, especially since she's going to be your maid of honor."

Amy smiled. "She's a great friend. She's always been there for me, through thick and thin."

Ted took her hand. "I promise to be there for you, too, Amy, through thick and thin."

As they neared the airport, a plane roared overhead on its approach for a landing. Ted looked up. "It's a great day for flying."

Amy laughed. "No day is a great day for flying. But, if one must fly, it's certainly better to fly on a sunny day."

Ted found a parking spot close to the Alitalia terminal. He turned off the ignition and looked at Amy. "I have a little going-away present for you."

Her eyes lit up. "You do?"

"Yes." He pulled the little black box from his shirt pocket and handed it to her.

"What's this?"

He smiled. "Open it and find out."

She gave him a sidelong glance and then slowly opened the box. At the sight of the diamond ring, her tears began to flow. "Oh, Ted!" She looked up at him, her eyes glistening in the morning sunlight. "It's beautiful. Absolutely beautiful!"

"May I?" He reached toward the box to remove the ring and slipped it onto her ring finger. "Amy Torelli, will you marry me?"

"Yes, Ted McMasters. I will marry you."

He slipped the ring on her finger and kissed her. "I was worried you might not like it."

"I love it, especially because it came from you." She admired the ring on her hand. "It fits perfectly."

He leaned over and kissed her again. And all the love in his heart flowed through that kiss. "I don't know what I'm going to do without you here."

"You'll be fine." But her voice betrayed her doubts.

"I'll join you as soon as I can. Meanwhile, start on our wedding plans. Anything you can arrange without having a definite date yet."

"I will." Her gaze locked onto his. "I'll be praying about the court case. Keep me posted on all the details."

He swallowed hard as he glanced at his watch. "Well, I guess we'd better get into the terminal so you can go through the check-in process."

"Yeah. I guess so." She didn't seem at all eager to leave.

He helped her out of the car and carried her luggage into the terminal. The check-in line was already long.

"I'd better get in line so I won't miss my flight."

Ted took her into his arms and kissed her again. "As long as I'm on this earth, I'll never leave you nor forsake you."

The look in Amy's eyes told him she understood. And not only understood, but also believed.

* * * *

The next morning, Amy sat in Mr. Conklin's office, the audit report resting on his desk.

"Amy, I must commend you on an absolutely outstanding job. I knew I could count on you."

"Well, I must say it was quite an adventure." She then proceeded to give him the details of the embezzlement, the deceptive ways of Silvia and Giorgio, and the near-death run-in with Mafioso Roberto Manero.

"All in a day's work, right?" Mr. Conklin laughed.

Amy laughed, too. It was easy to laugh when one wasn't in the thick of things.

"Seriously, though, you've brought honor to Enson and to yourself. I'm going to set you up for a promotion."

Amy hesitated. Should she tell him now about her engagement to Ted or wait until later?

"Um, Mr. Conklin."

"Yes?"

"I have something to tell you."

He gave her a questioning look and waited.

"Do you remember suggesting that I challenge Ted McMasters to a game of tennis?"

The elderly gentleman chucked. "Yes."

"Well, I did more than that."

He leaned back in his chair and folded his arms, a look of great interest on his face. "Oh?"

"Yes, I challenged him to a lifetime together." She let the words fly from her heart. "Ted and I are engaged to be married."

Mr. Conklin rose and came around to give her a hug. "Well, congratulations, my dear. Ted is a very blessed man."

"Thank you. And I am a very blessed woman. As you know from his letter, Ted has wanted to be a pastor for a long time. And I've wanted to leave the grind of the corporate world for a simpler life. So, we're planning to move to Texas to pastor a tiny church in our hometown area."

Mr. Conklin smiled broadly. "I believe you're both making a wise decision. While I will hate to lose both of you, I pray God's blessings on your marriage and your life together."

"Thank you, sir."

"When is the big date?"

"We haven't set it yet because of the court case."

"Well, you both will have your jobs until you need to leave. That's settled."

Amy's heart swelled. "I can't thank you enough, sir."

"Don't thank me." He pointed heavenward. "Thank the good Lord Who loves us so much and gives us every blessing."

"Yes. He certainly does."

* * * *

A week after Amy 's departure, Ted stood forlorn in front of the TV in his apartment. Still no word on the date of the court case. He was getting antsy.

Plus, his job now posed new challenges due to his strained relationship with Silvia and Giorgio. They hardly spoke to him except for absolutely necessary exchanges. He'd thought of leaving Enson and finding a temporary job, but doing so might create additional challenges he wasn't emotionally ready to handle at the moment. Better to stay put and get the whole thing over with and behind him.

The ring of his cell phone drew him out of his thoughts. The ID showed the name of Ted's defense attorney in the embezzlement case.

"Ted McMasters here."

"Mr. McMasters, this is Giovanni Testa. Sorry to call you at ten o'clock at night. I just got home from the office."

"Yes, I recognize your name, Mr. Testa. How are you doing?"

"Doing great on my end. How about you?"

"As well as can be, under the circumstances. I hope you're calling me to tell me that the date of the court case has been set."

Giovanni laughed. "No. I'm calling you for something far better than that."

Ted was all ears.

"I'm calling to tell you that your witness won't be needed in the case after all. Your tracker watch data proved your innocence beyond question. But, even more significantly, the identifying data—that is, the username, time, and date of all the fraudulent entries—embedded in the computer log and that made it look as though you had made the fraudulent entries, all carried the same date and time. And the date conflicted with the date on the ledger. Which proves that someone logged on with your username and password and altered the entries."

Mr. Testa continued. "We also have conclusive evidence from one of the custodians who vouched that Silvia was in the computer room on the date and the time embedded on the disk. He said she had complained to him about the noise of the vacuum cleaner. When all this information was presented to Silvia and Giorgio earlier today, they took the advice of their attorneys and confessed their guilt. So, there will be no trial."

Ted fell laughing onto his couch. "Are you serious?"

"Very serious."

"This is the best news you could have given me."

"I'm glad. You can now make plans to return to the States and proceed with marrying that fiancée of yours."

Tears welled up in Ted's eyes.

"By the way, she's quite the auditor to have discovered such an extensive international embezzlement scheme. You must be very proud of her."

"I am."

"Well, my friend, I wanted to let you know the good news. You can start packing your bags and moving on with your life."

"*Tante grazie!* Thank you so very much. You have no idea what your phone call has done for me."

Mr. Testa laughed. "Anything for the sake of love."

Ted ended the call and took a deep breath. He needed to call Amy right away.

Chapter Nineteen

As Amy prepared to wrap up the work day, the ring of her cell phone interrupted her. She looked at the caller ID. It was Ted. She quickly tapped the ACCEPT button. "Ted, are you all right?"

Ted laughed. "I'm great. And better than great!"

Her pulse rate increased. "What's up?"

"You'll never guess."

She couldn't bear a guessing game at the moment. "Tell me!"

"I'm coming home!"

"You're what?"

"I'm coming home!"

"You mean the court case is over?"

"No, it's going to be dismissed. My tracker watch data proved my innocence, so the defense attorney no longer needs my witness. But even better than that, Silvia and Giorgio confessed. So, the case was dismissed."

Amy drew in a deep breath. "Oh, Ted. God has given us another miracle." She got up from her desk chair and plopped down on the sofa in her office. "Praise His Holy Name!"

"Amen! I've booked a flight for Saturday morning and will be back in New York early Saturday afternoon. Will you pick me up at the airport?'

"Of course!" The thought of holding Ted in her arms once again thrilled her. "So, what happened to Silvia and Giorgio?"

Ted's voice grew somber. "When they heard that the evidence against them was so overwhelming, they confessed. Silvia surrendered to the authorities, and Giorgio, I'm heartbroken to say, committed suicide."

Amy gasped. "Oh, how awful!"

"Yes. It's terrible. Roberto Manero and his men were caught

red-handed by Interpol and now face charges of kidnapping, assault, and possible embezzlement. It looks as though they'll be going to prison."

"I'm glad they were apprehended. That will keep them from doing more harm."

"Yes, I agree." Ted paused. "Before I leave, I'm going to visit Silvia. I want to tell her I forgive her, and I want to tell her about Jesus."

"Yes. Do that! While she's still alive, she still has the opportunity to receive eternal life. Too bad Giorgio gave up that opportunity."

"I can't wait to see you, sweetheart, and to hold you in my arms. Once I get back, we'll set a date for our wedding and then plan our move to Texas."

Amy's heart thrilled at the prospect of starting life in a small, quiet Texas town with the love of her life, Pastor Ted McMasters. "Sounds great! See you on Saturday, sweetheart."

Amy ended the call and leaned back on the sofa. Ted would be home soon. Another miracle.

God's goodness had no end.

* * * *

After Ted's phone call, Amy had trouble concentrating. She sat back on the sofa, her mind reviewing over and over again their recent conversation. When she'd left for Italy four weeks before, she'd had no idea what lay ahead. Now that she looked back, she saw the hand of God in her life.

He'd always been there for her. Even during the worst times. Even when Daddy abandoned her. Even when Mama died. Even when she'd initially rejected Ted's love.

Resting her head on the back of the sofa, she closed her eyes as her life passed before her. God had given her miracle after miracle over her lifetime. But her pain had kept her from recognizing those wonderful miracles. Now that the Lord had opened her eyes, she could not thank Him enough. Not only had He given her Ted, He'd given her Himself.

* * * *

Silvia sat alone in the prison cell, tears flowing down her cheeks. Never had she felt so rejected, so abandoned, so alone. Of course, her own choices had brought her to this place. If only she could go back and live her life over again.

If only. If only. If only.

When her attorney presented her with the irrefutable evidence of Ted's tracker watch, the computer log, and the custodian's testimony, she had no excuses left. Everything pointed to her guilt. Her attorney had advised her to confess and, thereby, to shorten her prison sentence. She'd complied.

But now, sitting alone in the dingy cell, she wished she'd ended her life as Giorgio had. Then her misery would be over.

The guard came up to her cell. "Miss Villano, you have a visitor."

Silvia looked up in surprise. "A visitor?" Who would want to visit her? Who even knew she was in prison?

"Yes. A Mr. Ted McMasters."

Ted approached the cell.

At the sight of Ted, an overwhelming sense of shame shadowed Silvia's heart.

"Hello, Silvia."

"Hello, Ted." She averted her eyes. "Why did you come?"

"For two reasons. One is to say goodbye."

She looked up. "Goodbye?"

"Yes, I'm going back to America."

"I'm happy for you."

"Thank you. I'm going to become a pastor."

She nodded and gave him a weak smile. "I'm not surprised."

Ted smiled back. "I've also come to tell you that I forgive you."

She looked puzzled. "After what I tried to do to you, you forgive me? Why?"

"Because Jesus forgave me."

Her eyes filled with tears.

"And He wants to forgive you, too. Will you let Him?"

She hesitated. "Why would He want to forgive me?"

"Because He loves you and wants to have a personal relationship with you."

She looked up, tears welling in her eyes. "With me? Why would He want a relationship with me? I'm nothing but dirt."

"Oh, no, Silvia. You're not dirt in God's eyes. You're His precious creation. He died for you."

With tears rolling down her cheeks, her mind drifted back to the Crucifix hanging in her grandmother's bedroom. Her Nonna's words came flooding back to her. "Silvia, my little one, never forget that Jesus died for you to pay the price for your sins, because He loves you."

Could it be possible that Jesus loved her? Silvia Villano? The horrendous sinner who'd lived only for her own selfish ambition? Who hadn't cared whom she hurt along the way to achieving what she wanted? Could it be possible?

"Silvia, Jesus is waiting to take you into His arms. Won't you accept His love for you? He wants to forgive you and to welcome you into His family."

She remained silent, pondering Ted's words. "He wants me in His family?"

"Yes, Silvia. He wants you."

Silvia had always wanted a family. More than anything else in the world, she'd wanted a family. Now the God of the universe was inviting her into His family.

Overwhelming love flooded her soul. "How can I become a part of God's family?"

"You have only to accept His invitation. Say yes to Jesus, and you will be welcomed into God's family."

Silvia rose, approached the prison bars, and grabbed hold of them. "I want to be a part of God's family. I say yes to Jesus."

As the tears flowed from her eyes, she felt Ted's hand on her head, blessing her as her heart filled with the peace that passes all understanding.

For the first time in her life, Silvia knew she belonged.

Chapter Twenty

Four *months later . . .*

When Amy Torelli was a little girl, she'd promised herself that if she ever got married, she'd have a Christmas wedding.

And now her dream was coming true.

Anticipating her union with Ted McMasters, the love of her life, she waited with Sara in the small room behind the sanctuary. It would be a small wedding. A quiet one. Just the way she liked things.

"Are you nervous?" Sara adjusted the train on Amy's wedding gown.

"Yes." Amy fingered her mother's pearls lacing her neck.

"You look lovely." Sara smiled.

"Thank you. So do you."

"I'm glad you chose a tea-length gown for me. Now I can wear it to other events."

"You're welcome. You know me. I'm practical."

"Yes. So practical that you fell in love in Italy." Sara gave Amy the look.

"Must you always say 'I told you so'?"

Sara shook her head. "I didn't say a word."

"You're right. You didn't. Your look said it all." Amy laughed.

The sound of people entering the church caught her attention. These were the dear people of the congregation Ted would be pastoring. This was their new home church. What better way to celebrate their wedding than to share the celebration with their new congregation?

Amy opened the door to the sanctuary a crack and peeked through. The little church in the town of Odessa looked like a picture postcard. Handmade wreaths decorated with red bows and holly berries hung on the walls, while votive candles flickered along the altar railing. In the background, the church organist played a soft medley of hymns in preparation for the grand entrance piece of Pachelbel's *Canon in D*.

Amy gently closed the door. "The church is almost full. Ted and his brother should be here by now. The ceremony starts in five minutes."

Sarah adjusted Amy's veil. "Not to worry. Ted's brother is a responsible best man. He assured me last night at the rehearsal that he'd make sure Ted got here on time."

A knock on the door drew Amy's attention. She opened the door to allow Mr. Conklin to enter. He had graciously agreed to walk Amy down the aisle and give her away to Ted. She gave Mr. Conklin a grateful smile.

A pang of sorrow struck Amy's heart. If only Daddy hadn't left. He'd be giving her away today. What had happened to him? Was he still alive? Would she ever know? It was one of those things too heavy to carry, so she'd given it over to the Lord. Something she'd learned to do during her time in Milan.

Her sorrow over her father lingered but for a brief moment. Then a smile broke out in her heart. *You're my Father now, Lord.*

The organist intoned the wedding march.

Mr. Conklin offered Amy his arm. "Time to go." He smiled.

She smiled in return and took his arm.

Sara walked ahead, and Amy and Mr. Conklin followed behind.

As Amy made her way down the aisle, the smiling faces of the congregants warmed her heart. Ted's mother had a radiant smile on her face as she held Callie in her arms and watched Amy walk down the aisle. Amy smiled back and looked forward to many years of Ted's mom's famous Texas brew.

But there was one smiling face she sought most of all and upon whom her gaze settled. The face of her beloved Ted.

He stood at the altar waiting eagerly for his bride, a nervous smile on his face.

Mr. Conklin gently removed Amy's hand from his arm and placed it in Ted's. "Ted, I present to you your beloved."

As Ted took Amy's hand in his, joy filled her soul. God had proven Himself trustworthy yet again.

Holding Ted's hand, Amy turned toward the altar before Pastor Bentley Moore, the retiring pastor of the church, whom Ted would be replacing.

The beautiful words from the second chapter of the Song of Solomon flooded her mind: "My beloved is mine, and I am His." Yes, she was Ted's beloved. But most of all, she was God's beloved.

And that was the greatest miracle of all.

THE END

Praise for the Fiction of MaryAnn Diorio

In Black and White - A Novel

"*In Black and White* is an incredible story of how persistence in the face of oppression and prejudice conquers hatred and sinful behavior. The story is beautifully written, and incorporates humor throughout while tackling the difficult subject matter of racism. The characters of Jeb and Tori were thoughtfully and deeply developed, and the historical aspects of the novel were spot on!"

I read this book straight through in a few days! I highly recommend for anyone who is interested in historical romance or the interplay of interracial relationships.~ *Jules, Avid Reader of Historical Fiction*

In Black And White is inspirational historical fiction at its best. Centered around the interracial relationship between the protagonists, the author gives us a candid look at prejudice in the year 1959.

The lives of Jeb and Tori took me back to memories of my neighborhood in the early 1970s, as they faced persecution from family, friends, and strangers alike.

This is a story of faith and love triumphing over personal struggles of rejection and guilt, as well as the combined injustice that came from hate and fear directed toward them as a couple.

Separated not only by race and geography, Jeb and Tori managed to bridge the space between America and Ghana, finding common ground and enduring love through their unwavering faith in Christ.

For Christians and non-Christians alike, this book is well worth the time to read, and might even be life-changing for some.

An excellent read! I was given this book courtesy of the

author through Interviews and Reviews, and this is my honest review.

I highly recommend this book and would happily give more than 5 stars. ~ SwavelyKid, Avid Reader

What a powerful story! There are very few books that have touched me deeply…this is one of them. I am reminded yet again that forgiveness is one of God's most precious gifts. The story shows how deeply we can wound and hurt one another with our prejudices and false assumptions. But if we focus instead on serving our Lord, we'll find the peace that surpasses all understanding.

"In Black and White" is a great example of true love. "Yes, love had a price. And Love Himself, the Lord Jesus Christ, had paid that price."

What are you waiting for? "God's plan for your life is always better than your own." And this story might change your life :) ~ *Natalya Lahkno, Avid Reader and Book Reviewer*

" . . . be ready for a rollercoaster." ~ *Nicki, Reader*

The Madonna of Pisano -Book 1 of *The Italian Chronicles Trilogy*

"From the first couple of pages my emotions were pushed into chaos. I kept wondering at how easy it is for people to believe a lie and allow doctrine to be their truth …. This is one beautiful story that makes Christ the Redeemer shine so brightly." ~ *Reader of Fiction*

"Excellent characters, dramatic plot. Beautifully written, giving wonderful feeling for the setting in place and time. Emotionally intense situations, satisfying resolution. Among the two or three best novels I have read this year. Highly recommended." ~ *Dr. Donn Taylor, Novelist and Retired Professor of Literature*

A Sicilian Farewell - Book 2 of *The Italian Chronicles Trilogy*

"Such lovely writing—and an even lovelier story! Author MaryAnn Diorio takes her readers on a courageous journey, from the ancient romance of the Old Country to the perils and possibilities of the New Country. Well-developed characters and a story that will stay with you long after you've finished this enjoyable read." ~ *Kathi Macias, Award-winning Author*

Surrender to Love - A Novella

"I enjoyed reading *Surrender to Love* by MaryAnn Diorio. It was a short story that packed a powerful punch. Anyone who has ever experienced loss in their life, in any form, can automatically relate to the feelings of Teresa and Marcos in this book. In addition, there were three characters, each of whom experienced significant loss—but each from a different perspective; this brings even more depth to the book. It showcases how, despite knowing "what to do," it's not always easy to tell your heart to do what your head knows it should. And that saying goodbye can feel like a betrayal of sorts…letting go of the old is more than just head knowledge—it has to come from the heart, a full surrender." ~ *Cheri Swalwell, Book Fun Magazine*

A Christmas Homecoming - A Novella

Winner of the Silver Medal for E-Book Fiction in the 2015 Illumination Book Awards Contest sponsored by the Jenkins Group. "This short story is a wonderful way to start the Christmas season. It is a story full of human emotion and the struggles this life can challenge us with. The lesson throughout the story is that all things are possible through God's grace. This is a 'feel good' story that lifts the spirits and keeps you encouraging the main character to persevere and not give up. It is a great book for a short respite from our busy lives." ~ *Kimberly T. Ferland, Reader of Fiction*

"Well-woven. If only all stories made me sit on the edge of my seat, unsure of the outcome, but desperate for a good conclusion for the characters!" ~ *Sarah E. Johnson, Poet*

"A great Christian read. A powerful short story packed full of love, hope, heartbreak and a strong message on forgiveness." ~ *Jerron, Reader of Fiction*

NOTE: These questions may be used in a variety of ways, including book-club or reading-group discussions, in Bible-study groups dealing with the topic of unforgiveness, betrayal, abandonment, broken families, divorce, child abuse, other topics related to the division among human beings.

1. Amy struggles with trust issues because of her father's betrayal and abandonment. Have you ever been betrayed and/or abandoned? How did you feel? How did you handle the consequences of betrayal? What does the Bible say about the way to handle betrayal?

2. Children derive their image of God from their earthly father. When one's earthly father has been abusive or untrustworthy, one often has difficulty trusting God. What advice would you give to a person who has difficult trusting God?

3. When we are hurt, we often it hard to forgive? What is forgiveness, and what is it not? What does the Bible say about forgiveness? (You may wish to read my article titled "Deck the Soul with Boughs of Forgiveness" at

https://maryanndiorio.com/2017/12/25/deck-the-soul-with-boughs-of-forgiveness-2

4. Ted derived his sense of worth from his father. When his father belittled him, Ted sought his sense of worth in others. Why is it dangerous to look to others for our sense of worth? Who alone can give us our sense of worth and why?

5. People-pleasing is a common challenge among people. Why is people-pleasing a trap? How can we overcome people-pleasing in order to feel good about ourselves?

6. Silvia realized too late that she'd looked for happiness in all the wrong places. We tend to do the same thing. We sometimes

look for happiness in money, clothes, entertainment, trivial pleasures. Yet, all of these lead to a dead end. Where should we look for happiness? What, indeed, is happiness?

7. Having lost all hope once his guilt in the embezzlement was discovered, Giorgio committed suicide. Yet, he, like Silvia, could have repented and been saved. How can you recognize depression and despair in another person? How can you help someone suffering from depression and despair?

8. Ted knew from an early age that God had called him to be a pastor, yet Ted had not heeded that call. Instead, he'd gone his own way. Why is it important to discover God's call on one's life? Why is it important to obey God's call on one's life as soon as one discovers it?

9. Wendell Conklin exemplifies a man who brings God's Word into the marketplace. Some people separate the sacred from the secular. Why must we bring the sacred into the secular culture in which we live? What did Jesus mean when He taught that believers are "in the world, but not of it"?

10. As Amy and Ted drew closer to God, they grew closer to each other. This is a spiritual principle of particular importance to married couples. But the principle applies in any relationship. How can you apply this principle in any challenging relationship you may be facing?

Acknowledgments

Books are the fruit of the efforts of far more people than simply the author. Books are born from the combined efforts of many people with multiple talents, all of whom pool their resources to produce works worthy of readers. Such, I trust, is the case with this novel you are holding in your hands.

Above all, I would like to thank God my Father in Heaven for giving me the idea for this book. He is the Giver of every good gift. This story is a gift from His heart to mine. Thank You, Father, for entrusting me with Your gift. I worship You!

I would like to thank my Lord and Savior, Jesus Christ, for sustaining me as I wrote this book. Lord Jesus, You are the Awesome Redeemer, the Reconciler, and the Restorer. Thank You for redeeming me from sin and sickness, for reconciling me to the Father, and for restoring me to wholeness. I love You!

I would like to thank You, Holy Spirit, my precious Guide and Counselor, as You unfolded to me this story of Your heart. I could feel Your Presence hovering over me as I wrote. Thank You for guiding me on this creative journey and pointing me in the direction of Your choosing. I adore You!

Heartfelt thanks are also due to my superstar husband Dom who helped me with the grocery shopping, the cooking, and the cleaning as I worked tirelessly "in the zone." He also helped me with the research for this novel and did an outstanding job of proofreading and editing the manuscript. His input was immeasurable. Thank you, Sweetheart! I admire you, respect you, and love you!

Deep and loving thanks to my precious daughters, Gina Diorio and Dr. Lia Gerken, who prayed me through the tough times. I am so honored to be your Mom. You are the best!

Thanks also to my very smart son-in-law, Peter Gerken, a

computer engineer *par excellence*, who helped me make sense out of the computer technology so critical to this story.

A special thanks to CPA Nick Kennedy for his expert advice on the auditing process.

Heartfelt thanks go to my awesome Prayer Team--Dr. Adeola Akinola, Sandra Marrongelli, and Devata White--who stood beside me every step of the way, upholding me through the many trials that presented themselves during the writing of this book. Love and blessings to you!

Heartfelt thanks to Susan May Warren who coached me in the early stages of writing this story. Her suggestions on how to get to know my characters proved invaluable. Her encouragement inspired me to push through the challenges and finish the story. Thank you, Susan, for helping to make my dream come true!

A very special debt of gratitude goes to my amazing Beta Reader Team: Elizabeth Bråten, Sharon Lamson, Diane Werckle, and Ed Lane. Your input was invaluable in making this story the best it could be. Thank you for giving of your time and talent to help a fellow author.

Thanks are due also to my wonderful book cover designer, Hannah Linder of Hannah Linder Designs. Thank you, Hannah, for the stunning cover.

A very special thank you to Mary Kazmarck who suggested the title for the book. Thank you, Mary!

Special thanks also to The Diorio Champions, my private Facebook group of friends and readers who support my writing ministry with their love, friendship, and prayers. Thank you, Champions!

Last, but certainly not least, sincere thanks to my precious readers. Without you, this book would have no home. May its home be your heart. May it bless you and touch the deepest places within you with the redemptive, reconciling, and restorative love of Jesus Christ!

About the Author

Dr. MaryAnn Diorio is a widely published award-wining author of fiction for both children and adults. Her passion is to proclaim truth through fiction because only truth will set people free (John 8:32).

A widely published author of nonfiction as well, MaryAnn responded to God's call a few years ago to write fiction and has since published five novels: *The Madonna of Pisano, A Sicilian Farewell*, and *Return to Bella Terra*, all part of *The Italian Chronicles Trilogy; In Black and White*, winner of the *2020 Christian Indie Book Award for Historical Fiction;* and *Miracle in Milan*. She has also published two novellas, *A Christmas Homecoming* and *Surrender to Love*, as well as seven children's books: *Who Is Jesus?, Toby Too Small, Candle Love, Do Angels Ride Ponies?, The Dandelion Patch, Poems for Wee Ones*, and *Penelope Pumpernickel: Precocious Problem-Solver,* Book 1 in the *Penelope Pumpernickel Series of Chapter Books* for 7 - 10 year-olds.

MaryAnn holds the Doctor of Philosophy (PhD) and the Master of Philosophy (MPhil) degree in French and Comparative Literature from the University of Kansas, the Doctor of Ministry (DMin) degree in Christian Counseling from Christian Leadership University, the Master of Arts (MA) degree in Italian Language and Literature from Middlebury College, and the Master of Fine Arts (MFA) degree in Writing Popular Fiction from Seton Hill University.

MaryAnn lives in New Jersey with her husband Dominic, a retired physician. They are blessed with two lovely adult daughters, a very smart son-in-law, and six rambunctious grandchildren. In her spare time, MaryAnn loves to read, paint, and make up silly songs with her grandchildren.

MaryAnn hopes her stories will entertain and point readers to Jesus Christ, the Truth Who alone can set them free.

TopNotch Press
A Division of MaryAnn Diorio Books
PO Box 1185
Merchantville, NJ
FAX: 856-488-0291
Email: info@maryanndiorio.com

ALSO BY MARYANN DIORIO

The Madonna of Pisano

Book One in *The Italian Chronicles Series*

A young woman, a priest, and a secret that keeps them bitterly bound to each other…

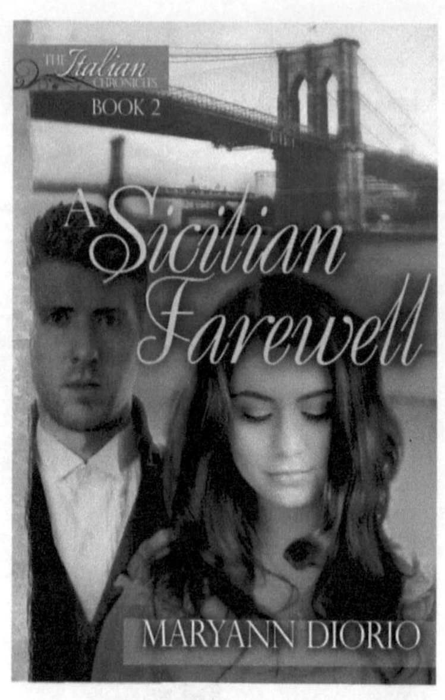

A Sicilian Farewell

Book Two in *The Italian Chronicles Series*

A young woman, a new land, and a dream that threatens to destroy her, her marriage, and her family . . .

Return to Bella Terra

Book Three in *The Italian Chronicles Series*

A mother, her son, and the man who threatens to come between them.

IN
BLACK
AND
WHITE
MARYANN DIORIO

Surrender
to
Love
MARYANN DIORIO

POEMS
for
WEE ONES
by MaryAnn Diorio
Illustrations by Valeria Wicker

DO Angels
RIDE PONIES?
MaryAnn Diorio
Illustrated by Valeria Wicker

CANDLE LOVE
by MaryAnn Diorio, PhD
Illustrated by Valeria Wicker

Written by
MaryAnn Diorio
The
Dandelion
Patch
Illustrated by
Doina Paraschiv

The
Penelope Pumpernickel
Series
BOOK 1
PENELOPE PUMPERNICKEL:
PRECOCIOUS PROBLEM-SOLVER
MaryAnn Diorio

MaryAnn's Social Media Sites

You will find Dr. MaryAnn on the following social media sites:

Website:

https://www.maryanndiorio.com

Authors Den:

www.authorsden.com/maryanndiorio

BlogTalk Radio:

www.blogtalkradio.com/drmaryanndiorio

BookBub.com:

www.bookbub.com/authors/maryann-diorio

Facebook:

www.facebook.com/DrMaryAnnDiorio

Goodreads:

www.goodreads.com/author/show/6592603

Instagram:

www.instagram.com/drmaryanndiorio/

Library Thing:

www.librarything.com/profile/drmaryanndiorio

LinkedIn:

www.linkedin.com/in/maryann-diorio-phd-dminmfa-99924513/

Pinterest:

www.pinterest.com/drmaryanndiorio/

Twitter:

http://twitter.com/@DrMaryAnnDiorio

Vimeo:

https://vimeo.com/user46487508

YouTube:

www.youtube.com/user/drmaryanndiorio/

Eternal life is a free gift offered by God to anyone who chooses to accept it. All it takes is a sincere sorrow for your sins (contrition) and a quality decision to turn away from your sins (repentance) and begin living for God. In John 3:3, Jesus said, "Unless a man is born again, he cannot see the Kingdom of God." What does it mean to be "born again"? Simply put, it means to be restored to fellowship with God.

Man is made up of three parts: spirit, soul, and body (I Thessalonians 5:23). Your spirit is who you really are; your soul comprises your mind, your will, and your emotions; and your body is the housing for your spirit and your soul. You could call your body your "earth suit."

When we are born into this world, we are born with a spirit that is separated from God. As a result, it is a spirit without life, because God alone is the Source of life. You may have heard this condition referred to as "original sin." Why is every human being born with a spirit separated from God? Because of the sin of Adam, our first parent.

I used to wonder why I had to suffer because of Adam's sin. After all, I complained, I wasn't even there when they ate the apple! Yet, as I began to understand spiritual matters, I began to see that I was there just as a man and woman's children, grandchildren, great-grandchildren, and so on, are in the body of the man and woman in seed form before those descendants are actually born. In other words, in my children there is already the seed for their future children. In their future children will be the seed of their future children, and so on.

Now, as a parent, I can pass on to my children only what I am and what I possess. For example, I can pass on to my children only my own genetic makeup. The same is true of my husband. I possess no other genetic makeup to pass on to them. And the same was true with Adam. Because he disobeyed God, his fellowship with God was broken. Therefore, his spirit died because it was severed from God. As a result, he could pass on to his descendants only a dead spirit—a sinful spirit, separated from God. And Adam's children could pass on to their children only a dead, sinful spirit. And so on, all the way down to you and me.

We said earlier that your spirit is the real you—who you really are. So what does it mean when our spirit is separated from God? It means that unless we are somehow reconciled to God, we will be eternally separated from him. That is what Hell is: a place of real torment resulting from eternal separation from God.

Now God is a holy God, and He will not tolerate sin in His Presence. At the same time, He is a loving God. Indeed, He IS Love! And because He loves you so much, He wanted to restore the broken relationship between you and Himself. He wanted to restore you to that glorious position of walking and talking with Him and enjoying the fullness of His blessings.

But there was a problem. Because God is infinite, only an infinite Being could satisfy the price of man's offense against God. At the same time, because man committed the offense, there had to be Someone Who would also be able to represent man in paying this price. In other words, there had to be a Being Who was both God and man in order that the price for sin could be paid.

Since God knew there was nothing man could do on his own to pay the price for his sin, God took the initiative. In the writings of John the Apostle, we learn that "God so loved the world that He gave His only-begotten Son, that whoever believes in Him shall not perish but have eternal life" (John 3:16).

What glorious GOOD NEWS! God loved you so much that He sent His one and only Son, Jesus Christ, to take the rap for your sins. Imagine that! Would you give your son to go to the electric chair for someone else? Well, that's exactly what God did! The Cross was the electric chair of Christ's day, and God gave His own Son, Jesus Christ, to go to the Cross for you!

In dying on the Cross for you, and in rising from the dead three days later, Jesus paid the price for your sins and repaired the breach between you and God the Father. Jesus restored the broken relationship between man and God. He provided mankind with the gift of eternal life.

So what does all of this mean for you? It means that if you accept Christ's gift of eternal life, you will be "born again." In other words, God will replace your dead spirit with a spirit filled with His life. "Therefore, if anyone is in Christ, he is a new creation. Old things have passed away; behold, all things have become new" (2 Corinthians 5:17).

If I offer you a gift, it is not yours until you choose to take it. The same is true with the gift of eternal life. Until you choose to take it, it is not yours. In order for you to be born again, you must reach out and take the gift of eternal life that Jesus is offering you now. Here is how to receive it:

"Lord Jesus, I come to You now just as I am—broken, bruised, and empty inside. I've made a mess of my life, and I need You to fix it. Please forgive me of all of my sins. I accept You now as my personal Savior and as the Lord of my life. Thank You for dying for me so that I might live. As I give You my life, I trust that You will make of me all that You've created me to be.

Amen."

If you prayed this prayer, please write to me to let me know. I will send you some information to help you get started in your Christian walk. Also, I encourage you to do three important things:

1) Get yourself a Bible, and begin reading it, starting with the Gospel of John.

2) Find yourself a good church that preaches the full Gospel.

Ask God to lead you to a church where you can learn His righteous ways of thinking and living.

3) Set aside a time every day for prayer. Prayer is simply talking to God as you would to your best friend.

I congratulate you on making the life-changing decision to accept Jesus Christ! It is the most important decision of your life. Mark down this date because it is the date of your spiritual birthday. Be assured of my prayers for you as you grow in your Christian walk. God bless you!